Submissive:

Tales of Love, Sex,

and BDSM

By

Audra Morgan

Submissive: Tales of Love, Sex, and BDSM

Audra can be contacted by email at

AudraMorganBooks@gmail.com

Books Included in this Collection

The Submissive Diaries Book One:

Kit's Awakening

By

Audra Morgan

The Submissive Diaries One: Kit's Awakening

Copyright © 2012 by Audra Morgan

Audra can be contacted by email at

AudraMorganBooks@gmail.com

Chapter One

I sat at my desk, trying desperately to shake off thoughts of the night before. A bit of role-playing and rough sex had suddenly transformed into something more, something neither James nor I had expected, and I wasn't sure quite what to make of it. I had a report to complete by four o'clock, and it wasn't going to be ready if I didn't stop fantasizing about how his fingers felt when they slid around my throat and squeezed just hard enough that I felt a little scared, or about the look in his eyes when I asked him to slap me harder. No, I had to get my head in the game, or my ass would be on the line…and not in the pleasurable way.

I closed my eyes tightly, attempting to will away the images of a candlelit room, set up perfectly for our anniversary, with various treats and toys carefully spread out on the bed. Massage oil, a satin blindfold, a glass dildo, and a riding crop were among the goodies that awaited me when we returned home from a romantic dinner at Muriel's. My stomach was full and happy after a dinner of crawfish crepes and bread pudding, and the after dinner cocktails had me feeling warm, and a little sleepy. The scene before me when I opened the bedroom door woke me right up. We had an amazing sex life, but James wasn't often this romantic. My interest was piqued.

Realizing that closing my eyes just made it worse, I focused on my laptop and began to enter numbers into the spreadsheet. 45 minutes until the deadline, and it was *not* looking good. I noticed the faint bruise on my wrist as I typed, and again my mind wandered back to the night before. Our clothes were on the floor within moments of getting home, and we fucked like mad without even giving the massage oil and toys a thought. An hour, and several orgasms, later, I reached over to the massage oil and picked it up, then lay back down next to him. "So were we going to use this, or what?" He laughed, then looked somewhat embarrassed. "I'm sorry. I'd had so much in mind for tonight, but I got a bit carried away. You just looked so beautiful tonight, all I could think about during dinner was tearing your clothes off and fucking you."

I smiled, happy that James was too distracted by thoughts of me to carry out his plans, no matter how fun they may have been. I popped open the bottle of oil, letting it pour over my hand, then I rubbed my hands together, climbed on top of him, and began to knead the muscles in his shoulders, arms, and chest. He looked surprised, as this

4

had not quite been the plan, but he relaxed into it and closed his eyes as he let out a soft moan.

Focus, I commanded myself. I could think about all this later. Casting off thoughts of my hands on his body, the sounds he made as I rubbed him, and *oh*, the things that came later, I took control of my brain long enough to hammer out the last of the report, give it a quick proofread, and email it to the director. *Done!* I silently congratulated myself, gave myself a metaphorical pat on the back, and leaned back in my chair, finally knowing I could let my mind wander at will. It was Friday, and an hour until quitting time, and I had a feeling this would be a weekend to remember.

Speaking of remembering, I thought back once again to the night before, and to the surprising turn things had taken once I was done with the massage. After grabbing a towel and wiping the excess oil off James' back, we lay together and engaged in a little post-coital, post-massage chit chat about various happenings of the day. After talking for a while, he grabbed the riding crop and playfully swatted my thigh with it. I smiled, then I asked him to do it again. We'd played around with it before, but he always seemed hesitant to go too far. Tonight, the look in his eyes told me he'd decided he'd like to change that.

5

James told me to flip over onto my stomach, and I complied immediately. "So you *do* listen sometimes," he remarked with a sarcastic laugh. I slapped him and buried my face into the mattress. He rubbed my ass tentatively, then he stopped.

"What's wrong?" I asked, turning to look at him. He wore a serious expression, as if something was weighing on his mind.

"Nothing at all. I've just been thinking a lot about our relationship, and about some of the things we've experimented with, and things we haven't, and I'd like to give some things a try." Never one to question trying something new, I turned back to look at him again, this time giving him a big smile.

"I'm game for anything you are," I replied.

"Good," he said, "I hope you don't regret saying that."

I felt his hand on my ass again, but this time he kneaded it almost roughly, then gave it a harsh slap. It felt different than the playful slaps I was accustomed to. I moaned involuntarily at the surge of sensations, and he took that as his cue to slap me again, this time even harder. He rubbed my reddening skin, then he took the crop and struck me several times in a row, from my thigh up to my hip. I cried out and he stopped immediately. "No, no," I panted. "I like it!"

With a swell of confidence, he resumed his work with the crop, this time on my other ass cheek. He swatted me again and again until I was out of breath and whimpering, with tears streaming down my face. The pain was very acute, and not something I was used to, but it felt good in a way that was inexplicable to me. All I knew was that I wanted more. It made me feel alive, and whole, and like I wanted to be his in a way I had never been before. As though he was reading my mind, he gently grabbed a fistful of my hair and pulled my head up off the bed. I instinctively turned over and sat up, and he pushed my head down towards his cock, which was standing firmly at attention despite the sex we'd just had.

"Suck me," he said with a tone in his voice I'd never heard before. It was guttural, raw, *bossy*. And I liked it. I took the tip of his cock into my mouth and swirled my tongue around it, then I licked up and down the length of his erection. He let out a little moan, then his hand was in my hair again. "No," he barked. "All of it." He forced my head down until my lips were pressed against the base of his shaft, and he moaned loudly as he heard me gagging. I didn't know how long I could keep that up, but I knew I wanted to try.

James pushed my head down as soon as I came up for air, and his cock rammed into the back of my throat. Tears streamed down my face, and I realized with embarrassment that I was drooling all over myself and the sheets. He didn't seem to care. Again and again he forced my head up and down, and I exerted every last bit of energy into not gagging, choking, or biting him. I felt his cock swell in my mouth, felt the telltale signs of approaching climax, and I forced my own head down onto him as hard as I could, holding my position with him pushing down into my throat.

"No," he said, pulling my head up, and he grasped his cock and pulled it from my mouth. He stroked it hard and fast until he exploded, and I closed my eyes as the warm liquid hit my face. Without even thinking about it, I licked my lips. "That's a good girl," he said as he watched me, and I felt a little bolt of electricity shoot through me as I processed those words. Yes. Good girl. I could be that. At least, *sometimes*. James grabbed a tissue and wiped off my face, then he collapsed onto the bed, pulling me down next to him and brushing my hair out of my face. "Did you mind that?" He asked, looking suddenly concerned now that the heat of the moment had passed.

"Oh my God, no," I replied. "I've been waiting for years for you to take charge like that." James smiled, almost sheepishly.

"Thank you," he said softly. "I'd like to do that more. A *lot* more."

For the next hour, we lay in bed talking about exactly what he meant by that. He was hesitant at first, but he soon discovered I'd been quietly curious for a long time, I'd just been afraid to ask. I knew he'd enjoyed bondage, administering pain, and being in control with his former girlfriend, but it wasn't something he talked a lot about. I was so strong-willed when we'd met, it was a no brainer for him to not even bring that topic up when we began dating. James lay next to me and told me how much he enjoyed our relationship, and how happy it made him, but he also said he'd been craving more of me, of *us*, and that he finally felt ready to make it happen. He grew even more serious as he told me he truly, sincerely wanted to take our relationship to the next level. He wanted to become my Dominant. And for possibly the first time in my life, I was speechless.

Chapter Two

We'd drifted off to sleep shortly after his bold proclamation. Before I could attempt to formulate a response, he'd asked that I sleep on it, and he said we could talk more about it over drinks the following night. As much as the thought had my mind reeling, the food, cocktails, and sex had rendered me exhausted, and I was out like a light in his arms in no time. But now, here I was, remembering every last detail of the night, goose bumps trailing their way up my arms each time I heard the word in my head. "*Dominant.*" I'd never even dreamed our relationship could take such a turn.

I was considered by most people I knew to be intimidating, domineering, and yeah, bitchy was probably bandied about from time to time when my name came up. If you looked up "submissive" on Wikipedia, I'm pretty certain you wouldn't find my picture and description. I'd dabbled in sadomasochistic fun with previous partners; I'd always been the sadist in the equation, and it was never something I got too seriously into. In the past few years, though, I'd come to enjoy being the recipient of a certain amount of playful pain. And although I'd have balked at it when I was younger, I was beginning to feel drawn to submission as well, the more I pondered it.

I began to think about the possibilities of truly being "his" in a way we hadn't yet explored, and it excited me a great deal. Perhaps it wouldn't work out; perhaps one or both of us would decide it wasn't right for us. There were really only two things I knew to be certain: I loved and trusted him completely, and the only way we could possibly know if this was a path we'd want to take would be to take those first few steps. He'd made it clear he wanted to take them, and I decided I wanted to give it a shot as well.

I powered down my laptop, thrilled that the weekend was upon me. We had a lot to talk about, and a three day holiday weekend was just what we needed. I'd never liked Independence Day; the fireworks enthusiasts in our neighborhood seemed to think they were obligated to indulge in three solid days of loud, smoky pyrotechnic madness. This wasn't terribly conducive to a peaceful holiday weekend, or to getting any sleep whatsoever. I'd always thought July 4th celebrations were meant to take place in the afternoon, with a barbecue grill and some beers, not with five thousand bottle rockets being fired off at two in the morning. Eh, what did I know; I didn't like barbecues either. I laughed to myself as I pondered how un-festive I clearly was, and I ducked quickly out of the office and headed to my car.

When I arrived home, I was disappointed to find that James wasn't there. I knew he'd taken the day off, so I'd expected he'd be home, waiting on me to arrive so we could indulge in our Friday happy hour tradition. Since shortly after we met, we'd spent nearly every Friday playing bingo at a neighborhood gay bar. It was silly, and usually quite corny, but we enjoyed it, and it was a fun way to kick off the weekend. Cheap and strong drinks didn't hurt. Well, sometimes they *did* hurt on Saturday morning...But I was determined to not succumb to a hangover this weekend. I had a feeling there was too much to look forward to to waste time with a headache.

I decided a quick shower was in order, so I tossed my laptop bag on the sofa and headed for the bathroom. I undressed, turned on the hot water, and hopped in as soon as I saw the steam rising. I leapt back as soon as the spray of water touched my behind; oh dear *Lord*, he really *had* given my ass a proper spanking with that riding crop. I smiled to myself and slowly backed up into the stream of water, laughing as it burned my skin and made me jump again. *Yes*, I thought to myself, *you are one sick puppy*.

12

I finished up my shower and pondered what to wear as I dried off. No matter how often we went out, it was always the same story. Ten minutes to shower and put on the little bit of makeup I wore, and thirty minutes to agonize over my clothing options. Bingo was in twenty minutes, and there was simply no time for that nonsense today. I threw open the closet door with a disgusted sigh, and hanging at the front of my overstuffed row of clothes was a note written on a torn-off piece of notebook paper. "Wear this. Be ready to go by 5:45."

I glanced at my cell phone, which was on the bathroom counter. It was 5:40. I grabbed the hanger the note was attached to; hanging from it was a simple floral knit dress, and on the floor underneath it were my favorite black boots, with socks already tucked inside. I threw my towel into the hamper and slipped on the dress, socks, and boots. As soon as I laced up my boots, I realized James hadn't put any panties in the bundle. Before I could consider grabbing some from my dresser, I heard the front door open. Time to go.

I slipped my phone into my purse and practically ran to the foyer. James was standing at the front door with a smile. "Two minutes early. This is something for the record books." He shook his head as he laughed, then looked me up and down. "You look beautiful. Ready to go?" We hopped in the car and backed out of the driveway, holding hands as we made the short drive to our favorite Friday destination. I suppose I'd expected to continue our conversation from the night before, but he said nothing as he drove. He simply held my hand softly, smiled, and sang along to the radio.

Butterflies rose up from my belly into my chest, and I suddenly felt like I might burst. I'd attempted to control my thoughts all day, to not obsess about the night before, about the implications of what he'd shared with me. But as I sat there, my hand in his, I wanted to turn the car around, go back home, and have a long talk about our relationship. Followed, hopefully, by more spankings and amazing sex. James clearly had other things in mind.

My "old" self would have spoken up and asked to go back home; I quickly realized my old self needed to shut the hell up and just go with it. Patience wasn't a virtue I'd acquired much of in my life, but I figured now might be a good time to work on that. It was nearly impossible, but I told myself to embrace the moment, and I squeezed his hand harder and smiled as my mind shifted to bingo, and to wondering what prizes we might win. *See, you can do this,* I thought to myself.

14

We drove around a while, finding it difficult to locate a parking spot thanks to the holiday weekend. We finally nabbed one, then we walked three blocks to the bar. James made small talk about the work day, and I bitched about struggling to meet my deadline. I didn't mention that the struggle existed mainly because I couldn't tear my thoughts away from his spanking me, fucking me, forcing my mouth onto his cock, telling me he wanted to dominate me. I blushed a bit, and James looked at me quizzically before sliding his hand around my waist and giving me a squeeze. I'd always absolutely hated having my waist touched; I almost slapped his hand away, but my new perspective on things gave me pause. Did I want to submit to him? Really? If so, I better learn not to flip out over a little squeeze. I had a feeling there would be *many* things I would need to get used to. He smiled at me again, and we made our way into the bar and to our favorite barstools, which happened to be unoccupied.

Bingo seemed to drag on. I usually found it pretty entertaining; we knew most of the regulars, and we always enjoyed our conversations with the bartender. This time, though, it seemed long and laborious, and I wanted nothing more than to get out of there, to go somewhere more quiet where we could talk. We'd each had a few drinks, so I knew he would open up to me, tell me what he felt, what he wanted, and I couldn't wait to do the same. The final round of bingo was called, and it was a blackout round. I stood up quickly, since we normally didn't hang around for blackout bingo; it was just long, boring, and pointless, as we never, ever won. James tugged my dress and shook his head. "The prize is a bottle of vodka - we're playing." I sighed, and he gave me a cross look. I mustered up a smile, grabbed my bingo card, and plopped back down on the barstool.

After what seemed like an hour of punching holes in the final bingo card, we left without that bottle of vodka. James was beaming anyway, though, and he suggested we head up the street to one of our other regular haunts. Once we arrived and ordered two more drinks, we made our way to the upstairs balcony. It was hot and humid, as July in New Orleans always was, but there was a bit of a cool breeze blowing, and it was nice to get away from the loud music and cigarette smoke for a while. Somewhere quiet, where we could finally, hopefully, talk.

James walked to the little table and chairs at the far end of the balcony, and we both sat down and stared at each other for a few moments before he cleared his throat and began to speak. He told me that he'd been doing a lot of thinking about our relationship, and our roles, and about what truly makes him happy. He said he didn't like to talk a lot about past relationships, but that his past had a big impact on who he was, the person he'd become, and that he felt a part of himself was missing, despite how happy he was with me. He'd just felt like he couldn't ask me to submit to him in any real way, that it wasn't in my nature. But recently he began to feel that perhaps it was something I'd enjoy, if only I was willing to give it a go.

I was all smiles, as it *had* been something I'd thought about for so long, since reading *Story of O* and *The Claiming of Sleeping Beauty* at the tender age of 14. Thoughts of dominance and submission intrigued and excited me, but I always fancied myself in the dominant role. And I'd never extended any of my own personal experiences beyond simple, harmless fun in bed. I'd also never felt quite comfortable with the idea of submitting to someone I didn't fully trust, so I thought it would never happen. Yet here I was, with the only person I'd ever trusted completely, and that's precisely what he wanted of me.

I was, as always, virtually bursting with questions. Was this just for fun, or all the time? Did he want to draw up a list of rules, or would we just talk it all out? Did I have veto power if I wasn't into something? He smiled and said we'd talk it all over, and we did just that. For hours, until we both felt like we were on the same page in terms of what we wanted, needed, and hoped for. His confidence and knowledge about everything astounded me; it was suddenly quite obvious the extent to which he'd been holding back a big part of himself.

James clearly wanted a lot from me, but he also wanted to take it slow, to be sure we didn't damage what we'd already built together. After hours of discussion, we agreed that starting right then and there, I'd relinquish a certain measure of control to him on a part time basis, and I would trust that he'd always have my best interests at heart, even if it didn't seem that way in the moment.

Giving up control to someone else was the last thing I ever would have imagined I'd be sitting in a bar happily agreeing to. I'd been a major control freak all my life, to the point that I'd lost quite a few friends and romantic relationships because of it. It had always been my way, all the time, and a big part of me finally understood how poorly that tended to work out for all involved. My job practically *required* me to be a control freak. Six people on my staff, and I often wondered if there was even one complete brain among the lot of them. If I wasn't constantly on their asses, things fell apart. The thought of being able to let a little control go was beginning to sound quite appealing. I wasn't sure how *much* I'd be willing to let go of, but I was definitely willing to find out.

We ended our long and interesting discussion with an agreement to give things a try for a month or so, and we promised to communicate as openly as possible with each other during that time. James admitted that he was somewhat uncertain of how I'd react to some of the things he had in mind, and I smiled and told him I was certain I could handle it. Seeming a bit more confident, he took my hands and asked if I was ready to begin. *Now.* My eyes widened, as I thought perhaps I'd have some time to mull things over a bit more, to mentally prepare. I realized that was my control freak self in action once again, so I took a deep breath and told him yes, I was ready.

James smiled, reached into his pocket, and pulled out a simple black collar. It was very understated, a thin leather choker, not something that the average person walking past me would even notice or find unusual. And it suited my personal style quite well. I was taken aback by the gesture, and my heart jumped a bit at the thought of the meaning behind this simple strip of leather.

"When you wear this," he said with a rather serious tone, "You're mine. Completely. If I ask something of you, I want you to do it. If I want to do something *to* you, *I will*. If something is ever too much for you, just take it off, and I'll know I need to step back." I processed what he'd just said to me, and it made perfect sense. I didn't see us diving into this twenty four hours a day, but a part time arrangement would work for us both. *And be a hell of a lot of fun*, I thought, a wicked grin creeping across my face. "And no being a brat," he added, noting the mischievous look on my face. "You're not going to get your way by manipulating me or intentionally misbehaving. *Ever*."

James slid my barstool closer to him, and he slipped the collar around my neck and fastened it. I reached up and felt the smooth leather, then ran my fingers over the small ring in the front. My face flushed as I imagined him attaching a leash to it and leading me around by my neck. I didn't think he'd ever do that, but it turned me on just imagining it. I was determined to let him run this show, though, so I would *not* be putting in requests. Besides, I thought, it meant so much more if it was his idea, and I couldn't wait to find out what schemes he'd been plotting. Little did I know, I was going to find out right then and there.

"So you're wearing your collar, and that means you're mine to do with as I please, right?" James asked me with a glimmer of mischief in his eyes.

"Yes," I said, suddenly feeling a little bit nervous. He looked around, noticing that no one else was on our side of the balcony.

"Get on your knees and suck me," he said softly. I stared at him as though he were speaking in a foreign dialect that I couldn't comprehend. I had no problem doing what he wanted, but I kind of thought it was something he'd exercise at home, in private. *Certainly not at a bar, where anyone could walk by and see us.* "Are you going to make me tell you again? I thought you understood how this was going to work."

I looked up towards the doorway to the balcony, noted that no one had come or gone the entire time we'd been there, and I stepped off the barstool and sank to my knees. The wooden balcony floor was hard on my bare knees, and I wished I'd worn jeans. *He picked this dress*, I suddenly remembered. He'd known exactly what he was doing. *Diabolical.* I quickly unzipped his jeans, and his cock practically burst out at me. By the look of it, he was most definitely excited about this public display of submission.

21

I held his cock in my hands and stroked it gently, then I took it into my mouth and began to suck him. He moaned softly. "That's my good girl, Kit," he whispered gruffly. There was that phrase again, and once more it gave me chills to hear him say it. I felt an unexpected surge of sensation through my belly and down into my pussy. I knew if he reached under my dress he'd find me wetter than ever. That excited me even more. I began to suck him with more enthusiasm, and he moaned louder, then he grabbed my hair and pulled me up quickly. An extraordinarily drunk couple had just stumbled out onto the balcony, and while they seemed almost completely oblivious, James didn't want to cause a scene. He zipped up his jeans, wiped my mouth off with his thumb, and said it was time to go home. We practically ran to the car, and we were home in no time.

I almost couldn't breathe as we walked into the bedroom. We'd been together for years, and we'd had all sorts of fun that most couples probably don't even consider. We'd had a threesome with a good friend of mine, and we'd even hooked up with a few couples over the years. I'd considered us a pretty liberal, open-minded duo, yet suddenly I felt like everything was new and different. We were in uncharted waters, and it was exhilarating and terrifying. The simple act of fucking had taken on a new meaning, at least while this collar was on. I wondered if it would feel different, if it would make *me* feel different.

Chapter Three

James walked to the iPod dock and pressed a few buttons, and Nine Inch Nails suddenly filled the room. "Happiness in Slavery" was the first song to play, and I laughed to myself, wondering if that was a coincidence, or if he'd made a playlist for the night. He turned to me, looking quite serious. "Get undressed," he said flatly. I was so used to our playful nature in bed, that this caught me off guard, and I wondered if things were going to all of the sudden become a bit too serious for my taste. As I disrobed before him, though, I saw that playful glint in his eyes, and I knew he wasn't going to remain serious for long.

Once I was fully divested of my dress and shoes, I hopped onto the bed. James looked at me sternly and shook his head. "Wow, Kit, you're an hour in and you're already giving me trouble. Did I *tell* you to get in bed?" He smiled, then he quickly regained his solemn expression. I jumped up and stood exactly where I'd been when I removed my clothing. "That's better," he said. "Now don't move."

I stood there naked, feeling vulnerable in a way I wasn't quite familiar with. I'd been naked with James hundreds of times, but I'd never felt quite like this. He sat at the foot of the bed and looked me over slowly, and I felt goose bumps spread across my flesh. We'd only just begun this journey, but things already felt so different between us, and the simple act of being made to stand nude in my own bedroom, without moving, cemented in my mind that if we were going to continue down this road, *everything* was going to change.

"Masturbate for me," he growled, finally breaking the silence. I looked at the floor around me, as if a chair would suddenly materialize. "No," he said, "right there, where you're standing. Lean back against the armoire if you need to. But I want you standing." I felt my face grow warm, and I still couldn't figure out why I felt so self-conscious. This balance of power thing was really fucking with my mind, and I was beginning to wonder if I could handle it for more than a day or two. I leaned back a little until my shoulders rested against the armoire doors, and I slipped two fingers between my legs, into the folds of my pussy.

I was quite shocked to feel that I was still wet. I surely didn't feel turned on; I felt somewhat terrified by my lack of control in the situation. I wanted to dive into the bed and kiss him all over, to throw my arms around him and tell him to fuck me hard. But here I stood, naked and a little bit cold, with two fingers dipping into my cunt as he watched quietly. Had I really asked for this? Yes, I suppose I had.

James unzipped his jeans and slipped them off, then sat back down on the bed, wearing only a snug-fitting t shirt. He looked so amazingly sexy, and I wanted to rip that shirt off of him and bite his chest, lick his stomach, trace his pelvic bones with my tongue. My eyes trailed down to his hand, which was slowly working his cock as he watched me. God, his hands...I'd always loved his hands. He had delicate fingers and smooth, soft hands that always felt so good on my body. I watched him hungrily, wishing he was touching me right then, but I'd have to settle for enjoying watching his hand pleasure himself. For now, at least. And pleasure himself he did.

His head fell back and his eyes closed, and he stroked his cock more rapidly, no longer even looking at me. My breath quickened and I rubbed my clit harder and faster, almost roughly, never taking my eyes off that hand. Without even realizing it was approaching, an orgasm overtook me and I cried out as my body shuddered against the armoire. James opened his eyes, looked at me, and smiled. "That's my good girl," he said, then he walked over

26

to me and kissed me on the forehead. I was so ready for him to take me, any way he could possibly want. But instead of grabbing me, manhandling me, ravaging me, he simply smiled and asked for a glass of water.

I was standing naked within his reach, my pussy soaking wet, still pulsating and aching for him, and he wanted *a glass of water?* I took a deep breath and made my way to the kitchen to procure his water. When I returned, he was in bed and had switched on the television. Surely he was joking around with me, playing a trick to see how much I'd go along with. But as I got closer, I realized he'd put on a pair of boxer briefs and seemed to be intently focused on some home improvement show I'd never seen. I handed him his water, and he smiled and thanked me. I got into bed and rubbed his leg, feeling his muscles tighten as my hand travelled up his thigh, towards his cock.

A hand pressed down on top of mine, stopping it in its tracks. "Not tonight," he said firmly. "I'll fuck you when I'm ready." Oh. Dear. Lord. He *was* serious. I wasn't getting any tonight. Without realizing I was doing it, I crossed my arms over my naked chest and turned my lips down into what was probably a rather unattractive pout. James looked at me very sternly.

"This…whatever it is you think you're doing here…is *not* acceptable. I suggest you get over yourself. The sooner the better." He returned his attention to the gripping account of someone's kitchen makeover, dialing the volume up a bit as he shook his head in what appeared to be complete disgust. He was clearly displeased with me. I felt the thoughts of anger over being denied fade away, replaced with a little guilt over acting like such a brat. I *did* need to learn my place, if I wanted to make this work. The question that I couldn't seem to answer at that moment was whether or not I *wanted* this to work. So far I'd been embarrassed in public and denied in private. Is this what all this was supposed to be about? I had to admit to myself, both experiences had turned me on, had made me feel a jolt of excitement that was somewhat foreign to me. Maybe that *was* what this was about. About my discovering a new part of myself, a new way to enjoy life, to enjoy him. I just hoped it would get easier. James rested his hand on my leg and gently rubbed and patted me, and I began to feel confident that it maybe it *would*.

Chapter Four

The next morning, I awoke to find James was not in bed with me. It was a three day weekend, which we usually celebrated by sleeping half of it away. My first thought was that I'd angered him, that he had realized there was no way I could be what he wanted me to be. What I'd *thought* I wanted to be. My hand fingered the collar around my neck, and I almost removed it. I decided I'd better wait and see what he had to say first. As I stretched and yawned before getting up, I realized I smelled bacon. *Bacon?* We normally scarfed down a protein bar in the morning, so the aroma of real breakfast was so foreign to me, I wasn't even sure if that's what I smelled. I got out of bed, threw on a t shirt and pair of gym shorts, and left the bedroom in search of the source of that perplexing odor.

"I thought I'd make us breakfast," James said with a smile as he placed two plates on our seldom-used dining room table. "Milk, or Diet Coke?" He asked, rolling his eyes at me.

"Diet Coke, of course," I replied with a laugh. I had no idea what the hell was going on, but the smell of bacon and eggs had ensnared me, and I was going to enjoy my breakfast no matter what. He pulled my chair out and made an overly dramatic hand gesture, indicating I should sit. He popped open a cold can of Diet Coke and set it before me, then he sat down and began eating. I had a few bites, which were, by the way, delicious, but I couldn't resist ruining it with my damned mouth. "So, uh, what's all this about?" James shook his head with an exaggerated look of disgust.

"Can we just enjoy our breakfast, Kit? Seriously." I nodded and cleaned my plate rather enthusiastically. I guzzled the Diet Coke and grabbed another one from the fridge, then I removed the empty plates and tossed them into the sink before sitting back down. James appeared full, happy, and ready to talk. I fixated on the "happy" part, as I'd feared the worst when I woke up. He scooted his chair a bit closer to me and took my hand in his.

"This isn't going to be easy all the time, Kit. It's not *supposed* to be. If it was, what would be the point? I want you to know I love you, and I appreciate *so much* that you are willing to try this with me. When I'm stern with you, it's because I need to be. Not because I'm mad at you. You *will* fuck up. I will too. Just trust me, and try to go with it, and it will be worth it. I promise." James was a man of few words when it came to "relationship" talk, so I was taken aback by how clearly and openly he shared his feelings about this with me. I realized he hadn't been mad the night before; he'd simply exerted the power I'd *given* to him. And he'd do it again.

I needed a serious perspective adjustment if this was going to work. I'd often felt guilty about how manipulative I could be, how often I figured out how to get my way despite what anyone else wanted. I'd felt like I should be a better person than that. But last night, I'd been on the verge of manipulating the situation to my advantage again, and when I realized I wasn't going to get my way, I resorted to pouting. How embarrassing. It was time to suck it up and do better. Dear Lord, I'd kind of thought this was just a fun way to spice up our sex life; I had no idea I was going to be thinking about all this serious shit, hardly twelve hours into our new arrangement. I laughed to myself, then I met his eyes with my own and nodded.

"I get it. Well, I *think* I get it. I'm going to try really hard. I want this too. I just think I kinda suck at it." James laughed and shook his head, then he grabbed my chair and pulled it until it banged against his. His hands scooped me up and dropped me onto his lap, and he encircled me with his arms.

"You *won't* suck at it. I just need you to work with me." He ran his hands through my hair, looking at me in such a loving way that I nearly cried. Suddenly my being denied sex the night before meant nothing; all that mattered was this. Being in his arms, being his, making him *happy*. And that's when it began to really hit me. All I wanted was to make him happy. I was ready to give up my self-absorbed ways and to make it my mission to make James the happiest goddamned Dominant ever. And what makes a Dominant happy is a good submissive. No, a fucking *great* one. I hadn't failed at anything in my life yet, and I wasn't going to fail at *this*.

"So," he said, "Will you wear your collar all weekend? Is that okay?" I smiled and nodded , wiping an unexpected tear from my eye. I relished the opportunity to have three days without the worries of work and "real life" interfering. I felt like I wanted nothing more than to spend three days showing James what an excellent job I could do of catering to his every whim, of pleasing him, of surprising him by how long I could go without being a total control freak. He kissed me gently, then slid his hand behind my neck and pulled me against him.

"I want you," he whispered gruffly into my ear as his free hand slid down over my breast and settled between my legs. My breath quickened, and I let out a sigh. "But we have some details to discuss first." I let out another sigh, but this time it was a frustrated one. "If we're going to do this right, we need to both be clear about what's expected. So let's get that ironed out. Then I'm going to fuck the shit out of you. He smiled playfully at me as he tickled me, knowing how much I abhorred being tickled *anywhere*.

We're going to make that against the rules!" I yelled out, swatting his upper arm.

"Oh, absolutely *not*," he replied wickedly. I half expected him to fire up the laptop and begin hammering out some sort of official contract. I knew people who had lengthy contracts drawn up detailing every little aspect of their Dom/sub relationship. I'd always found it a little silly, but then again, what did I know. To my relief, James remained seated at the table, and he didn't even grab a notebook. "Okay," he began, "we said last night that you're my submissive only when the collar is on, the rest of the time you're just Kit, my girlfriend, and I won't ask or expect any more of you than that. Does that still sound okay?" I nodded, and he continued. "When it's on, though, I expect you to do as I say, without questioning me or rolling your eyes or pouting, like you seem to enjoy doing." He smiled and ran his hand along my forearm, waiting for me to nod again. He was probably surprised at how quiet I was being; it was a rarity indeed.

"You and I have been together long enough that I think you can trust me to know what absolutely isn't okay with you. If there's anything that's completely off the table, though, I need to know. I'd like to you to write up a list and give it to me by the end of the day. We can discuss it if we need to. And as far as I'm concerned, if you don't put it on the list, it's fair game." My mind began racing through every possible request he might make of me; it was positively overwhelming, and I think that was quite obvious to him. He rubbed my arm, then took my chin in his hand and looked me in the eyes. "You don't need to figure it all out right this second, Kit. Just think about it today. I won't be mad if it's a long list. I just want to know if there's anything that crosses a line you're not willing to cross. God knows you're more liberal than most people, but I know you have your limits. I just need to know what they are." I nodded yet again, and he smiled. "I'm really happy, Kit. Thank you for this. I love you." I suddenly felt like I might burst into tears; what in the hell was *wrong* with me the past two days? I hugged him and kissed him, and he tilted his head in the direction of the bedroom. *Finally!*

34

I practically leapt off my chair and sprinted to the bedroom, and he followed me, a few steps behind, then caught up to me and grabbed my wrist before I made it to the bed. "On your knees," he said, with that serious look in his eyes again. I felt a little rush of excitement at being told what to do, at seeing firsthand how assertive he could be when he felt it was okay. There wasn't a hint of meanness, just a desire to be in charge. And by the wetness between my legs already soaking my gym shorts, I realized I was beginning to desire it too.

I sank to my knees and looked up at him, and he ordered me to open my mouth. As soon as I did, his cock was pushing into it, ramming the back of my throat as he grunted with pleasure. I looked up at him and noticed how different he seemed, how confident, how driven by pure, unchecked id. It was fucking hot, and I wanted him desperately. As he began to thrust harder, I gagged, and tears began to stream down my face as I tried not to choke. He looked down at me and stroked my hair. "That's my good girl," he said as he plunged his cock into me even harder, holding the back of my head so that I couldn't retreat.

I gagged and cried and thought I might be sick, but he wouldn't let up. I focused on breathing, on trying to get through it; he'd never fucked my mouth quite like this before. He slowed down a bit, then with a loud moan he pulled back and ordered me to turn over and get on all fours. He yanked my shorts down, just below my ass, rammed his cock into my pussy hard and fast until I was completely out of breath from screaming, then he exploded inside me with one last, hard thrust.

As I attempted to regain my ability to breathe, James informed me we were going to go shopping. *Shopping?* He had already disappeared into the bathroom, and before I could get up off the floor he was in the shower. "Get dressed," I heard him say from the shower. "We're going to leave as soon as I get out. You can shower later." I felt absolutely filthy and couldn't even imagine leaving the house like that, but I shrugged, washed my face at the sink, and threw on some jeans and a t shirt. Hopefully we wouldn't run into anyone we knew. James was out of the shower in no time, and he dressed quickly and told me he was ready to head out. I followed him to the car, trying as hard as I could not to ask where we were going. Once in the car, he looked at me in an almost admiring way.

You're really impressing me," he said, much to my surprise. I simply smiled back at him, not quite sure how to respond to that unexpected compliment. He drove us

36

downtown, and we parked right in front of a little locally owned sex shop that catered to the fetish community. It's where I'd bought my very first riding crop at the age of seventeen. The crop he'd used on me two nights before, although it seemed like much more time had passed since then. I had never gotten much use out of that crop, but I was suddenly very glad I'd bought it. Best $17.99 I'd ever spent!

James and I headed into the store, and I noted that not much had changed since I'd first been there so many years ago. It was a seedy little place, but it had just about anything you could ever want, and then some, in the two small rooms. One room contained what one might consider "basic" sex toys and items: vibrators, dildos, lubes of various kinds, and a small assortment of lingerie and porn. The next room over was slightly larger, and the lovely aroma of leather overtook me as soon as we entered. The walls were lined with leather corsets, harnesses, kilts, vests, and other clothing. Racks in the center of the room held riding crops, whips, floggers, paddles, ball gags, blindfolds, and all manner of restraints. There were other items I didn't even recognize, but it was all intriguing, and I wandered around, taking it all in. Things *had* in fact changed, and the toys had gotten a lot cooler.

James perused the leather restraints until he found something that seemed to appeal to him. He held up a pair of wrist restraints, and I walked over and held my arms out. I *was* getting good at this. Who'd have thought? He slipped the cuffs on and buckled them, nodding as he saw that they fit perfectly. He handed them to me and pointed to the rack. "Find a matching set of ankle and thigh cuffs." As I dug through what seemed like a thousand different leather cuffs, he looked over the selection of floggers and paddles. From the corner of my eye I saw him grab several items off the rack and leave the room. He returned, this time examining the various ball gags. I shuddered to myself, not even wanting to think about the possibility of his buying one of those. I'd always hated the thought of them, and I had never even tried putting one on. *That should go on my list*, I mentally noted as I finally located the ankle cuffs and moved onto my search for thigh cuffs. I didn't get the point of those, but he clearly wanted some, so I searched until I found them and marched over to him triumphantly, complete set of cuffs in hand. James took them from me and then pointed to the corsets on the wall to the left.

"Go pick one out," he said casually, still sorting through the horrifying selection of ball gags. I had quite a few corsets at home, but I didn't own a leather one, and I was pretty happy at the thought of getting one. I examined each one carefully, finally settling on one with zippers down the front. I already owned one made by the same manufacturer, so I didn't need to try it on. I figured I'd save that for when we got home. I handed it to James, and he nodded and walked back to the front counter with it and a few other items, one of which appeared to be a fucking ball gag. *Dammit.* James returned, grabbed a tiny leather item which I didn't think could even be legitimately called a flogger, and looked at me slyly. I nearly giggled at how silly it looked, and I wondered why a "serious sex shop" would sell something that looked like it would be found at Hot Topic for wannabes to buy in the hopes of looking cool. "Give me your arm," James said, tapping his hand with the tiny flogger. I rolled my eyes and extended my arm, sarcastic comments at the ready. He gently tilted his wrist back, then snapped it forward, and when the tiny leather straps made contact with my arm I saw stars and reeled back with shock. It *hurt*.

"What the fuck *is* that thing?" I asked, rubbing my arm as thin red welts rose up right before my eyes.

"It's a Torquemada," he replied, laughing. "Some sick Catholic monks created it during the Inquisition. Crazy, huh?"

"Yeah. Crazy," I said, glaring at the evil little monster. James smiled widely and walked towards the front of the store, still carrying it. *Definitely putting that on the list*, I thought as I followed him, still rubbing my arm and whimpering like a puppy that just got kicked.

James had asked the clerk to bag everything up as we shopped, so I was unable to see everything he'd bought. Diabolical, he was. He paid for our purchases, and as we headed out to the car, he stopped and turned back around to look at me. "You know what, I'm hungry. I think I want you to wear your new corset to lunch, though. Go put it on in the store, and then we'll go have some crawfish etouffee up the street."

I stood in the middle of the street, looking at James as if he'd lost his mind. My initial reaction was to slap him, then start walking to the restaurant. I quickly realized, though, that he wasn't kidding. Not even a little bit. He was trying to show me he really *was* in charge, and not just in our bedroom, not just for fun in private. He was testing me, and he knew how easily embarrassed I was. I'd thought we were taking things slowly, but it was obvious he had other intentions. I closed my eyes and breathed in and out a few times, trying to hold back the waves of a rapidly approaching panic attack. I opened my eyes when I felt James' hand on my shoulder. "This is New Orleans, Kit. You've gone out at night wearing much less. This shouldn't be a problem for you. Go change."

He was right. I'd gone out, albeit late at night, wearing skimpy outfits when we'd attended burlesque shows and gone to nightclubs. Something about walking around in broad daylight with my breasts front and center, though, just made me queasy. Sure, if anyone walked just three blocks up to Bourbon Street, they'd see much worse at noon on any given day, as they passed one strip club after another. Yet I felt so exposed at the mere thought of wearing a corset at lunchtime, when families and random tourists would walk by and see me, and wonder why in the hell I was dressed like that. At least I was wearing jeans and boots, and I wouldn't look like a complete whore.

I took a deep breath, grabbed the corset from the bag, and walked back into the shop to change. The clerk smiled at me and pointed to the changing room. *Goddammit. He already knew this was going to happen.* This mind-fuckery troubled me, and I suddenly felt confused and conflicted. I didn't know what to think. It had hardly been a day since

I'd thought this was the best idea ever, and already I felt myself wimping out, wanting to tear the collar off and go back to the easy life. It hadn't been bad, we always had fun, and we always had great sex. Why did he suddenly want to switch things up? And why did I so eagerly agree?

I slipped the corset on, and just as I realized there was no way I'd get it laced up alone, there was a knock on the changing room door. James came in, admired me in the mirror, then laced me up so tightly I thought my breasts would smack me in the face. "Can you breathe?" he asked, giving the cords one last yank before tying them.

"Somewhat," I replied, not feeling up to smiling or joking.

"Good. You look amazing." With that, he walked out of the changing room, and I followed. He tossed my t shirt into the backseat of his car, and we strolled up the street to the Gumbo Shop.

I simply loved creole food; it was just about the best thing in the world, and there was no other culinary delight I'd rather indulge in. It was, however, slightly difficult to enjoy with tourists leering at me, and with a corset laced so tightly I could scarcely breathe, much less swallow. It was like a tease. A gorgeous dish of jambalaya, etouffee, and red beans and rice in front of me, and I could hardly manage to eat more than a few bites. James scarfed down his plate of crawfish etouffee, then he tore off a piece of French bread. "Want some bread?" he asked, and I shook my head. I'd be bloated enough from all this rice, that was the *last* thing I needed.

James beamed at me as he enjoyed the last bits of warm bread. He looked absolutely...*effulgent*. Was my utter discomfort and dismay pleasing him that much? I never pegged him for a sadist, but this seemed awfully cruel and unusual to me. He was reveling in making me squirm, in pushing my buttons. Was this the same man who made me breakfast this morning? I couldn't reconcile this in my head, so I vowed not to think about it, at least until later, when it was time to sit down and compile my list of things I wouldn't allow, couldn't tolerate. The mental list seemed to be growing by the minute.

I asked for a to-go box, and I dumped practically the entire platter of food into it, certain I'd devour it later, once I could breathe again, in a t shirt and pajama pants without a brigade of onlookers judging me. James paid the waitress, and we made our way back to the car. He took my hand in his and smiled at me, leaning in and kissing my earlobe. "Thank you, Kit," he said quietly, then he said nothing more until we arrived home. I put my leftovers in the fridge, then I practically ran to the bedroom to get changed out of the corset. Once I was in my pajamas, I ventured back out into the living room, where James was on the sofa, checking email on his laptop.

Part of me wanted to sit next to him and nestle into his shoulder, and part of me wanted to throw something at him and then storm theatrically out of the room. I decided to compromise and have a seat on the sofa opposite him. I messed around on my phone, checking a few emails, then playing a game, not really knowing if I should say anything to him, or perhaps just wait for him to say something.

A bit of time passed, and James hadn't even looked up from his laptop. I cleared my throat in a rather lame attempt to get his attention. He looked up at me incredulously, and I suddenly felt quite foolish. "Shouldn't you be working on that list?" He asked nonchalantly. I imagined throwing my phone at him, and I immediately caught myself thinking negative things for the fifth or sixth time that day. I didn't know why I was so pissed off. I'd agreed to this. Why was it making me mad to go along with his requests? I nodded my head quietly, then decided I'd rather sit in bed and work on the list. Maybe I could think more clearly if I had a little alone time.

Chapter Five

I went into the bedroom, scrounged around for a
notebook and some paper, and dove under the covers. It
was so hard to think of what my limits were, when at that
moment everything seemed to be pushing my buttons and
crossing lines I didn't want to cross. But he needed a list. I
didn't want to come off like a total wuss; he'd known me
for years, and he knew I was a strong woman. Despite my
discomfort with the events of the day, I resolved to narrow
it down to the bare essentials. The things I absolutely knew
I could not do if he asked them of me. I was rather
impressed with myself when I discovered the list was quite
short. No public nudity or sex, unless it was in a bar setting
where no children might come along. No being burned (I
shuddered silently at the mere thought of it). No
humiliating me in front of people we know. I felt the urge
to scrawl out dozens more things on the page – no
withholding sex from me, no making me wear corsets to
lunch, no ball gags, no more of that hideous little tool of the
Inquisition. But I realized I need to bend a little. Maybe
even a lot. And most of all, I needed to trust him. Right
now, that was the hard part.

I'd experimented in the past with various forms of pain, and I was actually quite eager to give them, and others, a try with him. I knew he'd stop whatever he was doing if I used a safe word, so I truly felt I'd be okay with most things. Burning was the one thing I'd been afraid of all my life; whenever I inadvertently picked up a hot pan without an oven mitt, or drank soup that was too hot, I whined like a baby for hours. If my skin blistered, I was insufferable for days. I couldn't imagine *ever* bringing that into our play time and liking it one bit. And I simply wasn't willing to engage in sex or nudity in public places where kids or cops might wander by; if anything was a hard limit for me, that was it. Sure, we lived in the land of baring breasts for beads; but that wasn't me, and I wasn't going to partake of that in parks or shopping malls or restaurants, for him or for anyone else. At a private party, sure. I'd done it before. And even in a secluded corner of a bar; hell, I'd done it just last night. But nowhere I could get arrested, or have a child see me. And I *definitely* knew I had to draw the line at being embarrassed in front of friends. I'd been so uncomfortable sitting at lunch in that damned corset, that any intentional effort to cause me embarrassment around people I knew would most assuredly send me spiraling over the edge. I just couldn't handle it, period. I hoped James would understand these three limits, and that he would respect my wishes. If he couldn't, then we'd very likely find ourselves at an impasse.

I tore the sheet of paper out of the notebook, climbed out from under the covers, and returned to the living room. I'd calmed down a bit, so I sat next to James and handed him the paper. He raised an eyebrow when he noticed that the page was nearly blank. *"Really?"* He asked. "This is it?" He read it over, then set the paper down on the sofa and just stared at me for a long time. "Okay. No burning. No public nudity. Not a problem. You may need to work with me on that third one." I wrinkled my nose at him, not sure why he seemed to have an issue with not embarrassing me in front of friends. "Kit," he continued, "It's not that I intend to embarrass you. It's that, well, *everything* embarrasses you. And you need to work past that. I will promise that I will never set out to humiliate you. But if I ask something of you, and it happens to embarrass you, I want you to agree to try to work though it and do what I ask of you. If you can't, give me the safe word, and we'll move on."

I thought about that for a bit, and I realized he was right. I'd lived my life in fear of looking like a fool. I'd never sung karaoke when out with friends. I'd skipped out on group trivia games because I didn't want to be the one who shouted out the wrong answer. I'd sure as hell never taken salsa classes, or even art classes. Why did I always feel like everyone was looking at me, waiting for me to make an ass of myself? Surely people had better things to do than wait with baited breath for me to fuck up. He was right. I didn't like the thought of it, but I was thirty years old. It was time to grow up and get over myself. "Okay," I finally replied. "And by the way, my safe word is Unicorn." James laughed so hard he had a tear streaming down his face, then hugged me tightly.

"You're a mess, Kit," he said. "But you're *my* mess."

I spent the rest of the day running errands. We were desperately in need of groceries, and I'd decided I'd like to buy some new sheets. I browsed the selection at Target, finally settling on some black Egyptian cotton sheets that seemed like they'd do nicely. On the way out, I noticed some tealight candles were on sale. I figured they'd make for some nice mood lighting in the bedroom, so I grabbed two packages. James was working in the office when I got home, so I washed and dried the sheets, made the bed, and placed the candles around the bedroom. I heated up my lunch, practically inhaled it, took a shower, then sat down to read a book I'd downloaded. It was a primer of sorts on

48

all things BDSM, and as confused as I'd felt all day, I decided I needed it.

I read for hours, and my hostility softened quite a bit. I realized James wasn't trying to hurt me, to embarrass me, to be mean to me. He was attempting to establish our roles, and to break me of some of the controlling and domineering behavior I had been quite guilty of since we'd met. And since I'd agreed to this, there was nothing mean or abusive about his efforts; he was doing exactly what he *should* be doing. This was so much more complex than the bedroom-only role playing I'd done years before, tying partners up and smacking them around for fun during sex. This was hard work, and I had to trust that there would be a payoff.

By the time I finished the book, it was after ten o'clock. James had wrapped up his work (he hated having to work over the holiday weekend, but duty called), and he joined me in the bedroom. "Are you upset with me?" He asked, looking somewhat sheepish. I shook my head and leaned over to kiss him. "Good. Now take off your clothes." *Finally*, I thought. *Getting to the good part.*

Chapter Six

"I want you to understand," James spoke so softly it was almost a whisper. "When you are wearing my collar, I'm in charge. And whatever you do, you do to please *me*. If I decide I want you to receive pleasure, you will. But don't ever forget that I'm the one who decides that." I nodded. Having just read my handy BDSM primer, I felt like I understood things better, and I felt like I was truly ready to explore this world in earnest, without all the fussing and internal conflict. James smiled. "That's my good girl." *There were those words again.* I closed my eyes and leaned in towards him. He kissed me gently, then I felt the leather cuffs sliding around my wrist. He buckled them swiftly and hooked them together, and he flipped me onto my stomach. He fastened the cuffs to the headboard, completely restricting my movement, then he cuffed my ankles and fastened them to either side of the bed, so that my legs were spread and completely motionless.

I felt James' lips on the back of my neck as he slipped a blindfold over my eyes. He caressed my shoulders, my back, the base of my spine, until I shivered with pleasure. I felt him climb off of me, and a few moments later I smelled sandalwood incense and heard soft classical music. I smiled to myself, thinking that this was even better than our anniversary celebration. He returned to the bed, and I felt the familiar shape of the riding crop sliding along my side, almost tickling me as it reached my waist. I stifled the urge to laugh and scoot away from it; it's not like I could move anyway. He dragged it more roughly across my back, then he swatted me on the shoulders several times. That was a new sensation, and it definitely got my attention. My body came alive as I felt the crop strike me over and over, then after a brief pause, it made contact with my hips, my ass, my thighs. The fast, regular blows hurt at first, but after a while they began to feel good, and I caught myself moaning with each one. James must have taken that as a cue to stop; I heard him drop the crop on the bed, and then I felt the thin leather strips of that blasted flogger from the sex shop. He dangled it over me, tickling my lower back with the tiny strings of the Torquemada as I squirmed involuntarily.

"Be still," he ordered loudly, and I immediately stopped fidgeting. I heard a faint whir in the air as he snapped the Torquemada backwards, then forwards and onto my ass. My entire body lurched upward as the searing, stinging pain hit me, and James forced me back down onto the bed with his free hand. He flogged me again and again with it, and I felt tears streaming down my face although I tried my hardest not to cry. My entire body was on fire, I'd never felt anything like it before, and I didn't know whether I loved it or hated it. My nerve endings were sending me mixed signals, and finally I began to sob uncontrollably.

The leather nightmare was replaced by James' hands, caressing my skin as softly as he could, and it felt delicious. I moaned into the mattress, feeling a light, cool, tickling sensation over the sharp stings that covered my back, ass, and legs. As I lay there, I thought about subspace, which I'd heard about before, and read about earlier that night. I knew I hadn't "gotten there", and I was curious how much more pain I'd have to endure if I ever wanted to experience it. I wasn't sure I'd ever make it there, because I didn't think I could handle much more than that. The cool sensation of some sort of lotion on my back roused me from my thoughts.

"You're back is a mess, Kit, I'm putting some aloe on it." James gently massaged the aloe into my warm skin, then he removed the blindfold and unfastened my cuffs from the bed. He didn't remove them from me, but I liked the way they felt around my wrists and ankles. It was like the collar, but an even more obvious reminder that I was his, to do with as he pleased. I smiled to myself as I pondered sleeping with them still on, just in case he decided to have some fun with me in the middle of the night. James set the bottle of lotion down and flipped me over onto my back.

Oh my God. Pain. My skin felt like it was literally melting into the sheets. I was quite proud of myself for not yelling out "Unicorn" in the middle of the flogging. It had hurt like hell, but it had been strangely exciting, in a much more intense way than being smacked with the riding crop. I wiped a few remaining tears from my eyes as James leaned in to kiss me. "This will get your mind off your back," he said with an evil grin, holding a tiny green object in the palm of his hand. It looked too small to be a vibrator, but after he gave it a little squeeze, it began to buzz.

James teased me with the vibrator, running it along the inside of my thighs, moving inward across the folds of my pussy, but never touching my clit. My back arched, aching for some pleasure to compensate for the pain still coursing through my body. He laughed as he watched me struggling to get closer to those vibrations. "Patience," he said softly. "And you're not going to come tonight. Don't you dare.

No matter how good this feels." With that, he slid the soft vibrator right over my clit and held it there gently as my body began to convulse from the waves of pleasure that wouldn't stop crashing over me. I began to pant uncontrollably; the vibrations were too much for me, it felt too good, there was no way I could resist.

As I arched my back and moaned, James pulled the vibrator away from my body and slid his hand around my throat, staring almost menacingly at me. "You are *not* allowed to come tonight. I'm going to put this back on your pussy, and I'm holding it there, and I want you to control yourself. Do you understand?" I nodded, feeling the pressure of his hand bearing down on my throat. His hand almost choking me, and his threatening expression, nearly made me climax right then and there, but I took a deep breath and nodded again. "Good," he said, releasing my throat and turning his attention back to my cunt.

He slid the vibrator back over my clit, making small circular sweeps over my swollen pussy as I panted, squinted my eyes, balled my hands up into fists, and exerted every last bit of energy to keep the rising waves of pleasure at bay. My goal during sex had always been to come, and to come hard; I'd never been told I *couldn't* climax. It made me want it more, and the amazing vibrator he had pressed against me wasn't helping matters. I threw my hands over my face and began to cry for a second time in less than an hour. I thrashed back and forth under his hand, under that blasted vibrator, not knowing how to make it stop. "Breathe and be still," James said to me, removing the vibrator for a moment so I could catch my breath. "Stop fighting against it, just stay calm and keep from coming."

He may as well have been muttering in Greek; it made no sense. But I tried to do as he said. I took several deep breaths until I felt my body sink back into the mattress, and I lay there as still as I could, just focusing on breathing. James rubbed my stomach and my thighs, then he slipped his fingers into my pussy effortlessly. My God, I was drenched. He was expertly massaging the inside of my cunt, and it felt unbelievable.

As soon as he felt my breathing quicken, he slowed down the movement of his hand. "Just breathe, Kit." He then began to stroke me faster again, until my eyes rolled back into my head and my entire body began to tense up. "No, Kit, just *breathe*." I just let the feelings wash over me, amazed at how good his fingers felt inside me. With his other hand, he placed the vibrator back on my clit, and held it firmly as his fingers continued to work my pussy.

"Breathe. Don't come." I panted until I saw stars, and I thought I might leave my body. It was incredible. I'd had multiple orgasms many times before, and that last one was always a doozy, and it usually ended with me flopping around the bed like a fish out of water. This felt almost better, yet I found myself lying still, just taking it in.

James slipped his fingers out of me and switched off the vibrator, and I let out a deep sigh. "You can come tomorrow," he said quietly as he lay next to me, stroking me softly. I lay there, taken aback by the range of sensations and emotions I'd felt. I'd cried twice, I'd experienced pain like nothing I'd felt before, and my back and thighs still stung like mad. I'd felt pleasure that was almost unparalleled, and while I hadn't climaxed, I felt more satisfied than I could comprehend. I drifted off to sleep with what was most assuredly a dumb grin on my face.

Chapter Seven

I awoke the next morning to my phone ringing. It was my best friend Marissa, wanting to go shopping. *Ha, Shopping*! I imagined it wouldn't be as interesting as my shopping trip the day before, but I did need some new clothes for work, so we made plans for the next day. I kept my tone nonchalant, but I knew I'd end up telling her all about my exciting weekend, and that she'd most likely freak out a bit. Marissa was always giving me a hard time about the fact that we'd had a threesome a few times with my *other* best friend, before she'd moved away. I usually shut her up pretty quickly by telling her she was just jealous because it hadn't been her. She hadn't yet come up with a reply beyond merely groaning and slapping me.

James was lying next to me staring at me with a raised eyebrow, so I told Marissa I'd see her Monday, and I hung up. "Shopping? Again?" He asked, nudging me and smiling sarcastically. I asked him if he wanted *me* to make breakfast this time, and he laughed and rolled his eyes. "I don't think I want to spend my holiday weekend in the hospital with salmonella, Kit. A protein bar and some water will be just fine." Acknowledging my utter lack of kitchen know-how, I hopped up, grabbed two breakfast bars and some bottles of water, and returned to the bedroom to find James on the phone and in the midst of dressing. "I'm going to have to take this to go, Kit, there's a meltdown at the office and I need to run. I'll be back this afternoon. There's a party I want to go to tonight, we'll leave about ten." With that, he kissed my forehead and was gone.

So much for this fabulous three day weekend, I thought with a frown. James was anything but a workaholic, but his job had become a bit overwhelming in recent months, with lots of travel, late nights at the office, and on-call hours on the weekend. Neither of us liked it, but we were trying to take it in stride. I knew he had a work trip coming up, and I almost couldn't bear to think about it. We were going through such big changes in our relationship, and I feared having him gone would set us back before we could hit our stride. No sense worrying about it now, though, so I decided to go for a run, take a shower, and then do a little more research.

A run along the river seemed like a good plan, despite the heat, so I trudged up to the top of the levee and began to run, watching the barges passing on the river and thinking about the past few days. It occurred to me how funny life can be, how sometimes you don't realize what you want until it just sort of happens, and about how I'd never quite understood James' previous relationships before. A surge of jealousy swept over me as I realized he'd had a deeper connection with those girls than I'd been able to comprehend; perhaps deeper than he'd had with me all these years. I'd kind of assumed it was all just sexy fun and games, but now I understood there was another level to it, a psychological connection that extended far beyond the bedroom, far beyond sex.

I pushed away those thoughts of his previous encounters, choosing to instead focus on the now. I realized I'd struggled a bit; I'd been confused about his intentions, doubted the point of some of his actions, but it was making more and more sense to me. These new experiences we were sharing made me feel closer to him, and I really *did* want to push myself, even when it wasn't comfortable or easy.

After my run and a long, hot shower, I settled onto the sofa to do some more research. This time, instead of a book, I hit the web and checked out some fetish based social network sites. I read forums on every topic imaginable: spanking, age play, consensual nonconsent, Master/slave relationships, electricity play, and even one on submissives with an attitude. *Yeah, I liked that one a lot.* I decided to set up an account so I could continue following some of the discussions; I hadn't realized how *little* I knew until I browsed the forums and read post after post from a variety of knowledgeable and experienced individuals. I was also quite relieved to read and discover that submissive didn't mean "doormat" by any stretch of the imagination. Submissives had power and control; it just came in a different form.

I was particularly intrigued by the subject of the Master and slave dynamic, and how it seemed to take the concept of submission one big leap forward, releasing all control, full time, to an individual. I read about the various forms that dynamic could take, and I smiled to myself, imagining James calling me his slave, his pet, his owned property. It shocked me a bit that this idea even remotely appealed to me. Had I come that far in only a few days? *Nah*, I thought, *it's a great fantasy, but not for me.*

As I sat there daydreaming with my laptop, the front door opened, and James walked in with an exhausted sigh. I hopped up and gave him a hug, and he handed me his laptop bag. "I'm beat," he said, looking more like he'd been beaten *up*. "Today sucked. Can you make me a drink?" I lay his laptop bag down on the ottoman, then whipped him up a vodka with Red Bull. I knew there were party plans on the schedule, and he looked like he needed a pick-me-up. He smiled, kissed me, and practically chugged his caffeinated cocktail. I made him another, and when I returned, he was glancing at my laptop and smiling. "You've been a busy girl today, I see." I looked down, feeling a little embarrassed, but I didn't even know why. "So," he said, "find anything interesting?" I plopped down next to him and slid the computer onto my lap, then I pulled up one of the pages I'd spent a good bit of time perusing.

"This," I said with a grin. It was a site about violet wands, which I'd never even heard of before my day of research. But *damn*, they looked cool.

"Ah, getting hardcore on me, are you?" James said with a laugh. He told me he had a friend who had a violet wand kit with all the attachments, and he said that he'd seen them used at a few parties. Electricity was considered "edge play" among most, but James explained to me that the various attachments that could be used allowed for very gentle sparks of electricity that almost felt like being tickled, all the way through more extreme attachments that could actually brand the skin semi-permanently. I shuddered a bit, my fear of being burned taking over my consciousness. "There's a lot of middle ground in between the two, though," he assured me. "Frankly, I think it's something you'd enjoy." I shrugged, really not sure if my interest in this fascinating device was academic, or personal. It would be neat to see one in action, but I wasn't certain I'd actually want one used on *me*.

We talked a bit more, and then it was time to head to the party. It occurred to me I had no idea where we were even going. "It's perfect timing, actually," James said, a mischievous expression creeping across his face. "There's a fetish party tonight. An out-of-town group is hosting it; it's supposed to be pretty amazing." I found the proposition exciting, but also a little bit daunting. We'd been to a few parties like that in the past, just as observers, but nothing much had happened at them. This one sounded different, and well, *we* were different now. I wondered if he planned to take advantage of our new dynamic and have a little fun with me at the party. Part of me hoped he would, and part of me *really* hoped he wouldn't.

"So, what would you like me to wear?" I asked somewhat tentatively. While I wasn't used to asking what I was expected to wear, it was a bit of a relief not having to drive myself crazy figuring out what to put on. I was not surprised to learn that James already had an outfit in mind.

"Your new corset, one of your short black skirts, and your black boots." I rolled my eyes, as James knew I owned at least half a dozen pairs of black boots. He caught his error right away. "The knee high ones with the heels." I headed to my closet to retrieve those items, then called out for his help with getting the corset tied up. The horror I'd felt at the restaurant at lunch the other day was replaced with a smug smile as I admired the way the corset accentuated my figure. With each tug of the strings, my waist got smaller and my breasts swelled. I always did love to wear a nice corset, but the leather look was so different than the satin and lace ones I was accustomed to. After I was sufficiently corseted up, James helped me get my boots laced up as well; he knew there was no way I'd be able to bend over and get them on, and I appreciated his help.

I decided to put on a little more makeup than usual; with the leather corset, short skirt, and badass boots, I figured some extra mascara and red lipstick were called for. James snuck up behind me and kissed my neck, took a deep breath in, and told me I smelled delicious. It was time to head out, so we left, hand in hand, and as he drove us to the party he told me a bit about what to expect. There would be various stations set up throughout the party where experts at different types of BDSM play would be giving demonstrations, and there would also be plenty of space for the party-goers to play in whatever manner they chose. After my day of reading, I was quite excited to see what sorts of things would be happening. James informed me that he'd called an old friend and asked him to come by as well, because he thought I'd like to meet him. It sounded like a fun night, and I was anxious to get it started.

After parking, I hurried to the front door of the bar, aware of the fact that a good bit of my ass was on display for anyone who might be walking by. James caught up with me and paid the door fee for us both, and we headed in to find a spot at the bar. Dark industrial music played in the background, and we watched people slowly filter in for the party as we sipped our cocktails. I'd ordered a Long Island, and James said he would be sticking with Blue Moon; he didn't want to drink too much. Liquid courage now in my hand, I hoped that meant some fun was in store for us, but I couldn't help noticing he hadn't brought along any floggers or other goodies. Ah well, it would certainly be enjoyable and interesting to see what sorts of things others would be doing throughout the night.

"I think the fire cupping demo is about to begin," James said, rising from his barstool and taking my hand to help me off mine. My corset was so tight that I was a little off-balance, so I appreciated the assistance. We walked to the rear corner of the dance floor area, where a massage table had been set up, and a pale woman was lying, naked and face down, on it, waiting for the demonstration to begin. An unassuming older man carefully pulled small glass jars from his bag and placed them on the metal stand next to the massage table. He pulled out some cotton balls, some liquid in a bottle, and something that appeared to be forceps. I'd read about quite a few of the more exotic types of kinky play over the last few days, but I hadn't come across anything quite like this. I had no idea what was going to happen, and I couldn't help flinching at the thought that the poor girl on the table was going to be burned. Not only did I hate the thought of it happening to me, but I also didn't want to watch it happening to anyone else. I was too embarrassed to ask James, so I decided I'd just wait and hope "fire cupping" didn't actually involve setting anyone on fire.

Several people crowded around us to watch the demonstration, and I was pleased we were right up front. Even if I wasn't sure I wanted to see what was about to happen, I also didn't want to be stuck at the back of the crowd. The man slowly rubbed oil all over the girl's back, massaging it in lovingly. He then rubbed some of the oil on the edge of the glass jars. He poured some liquid, which James whispered to me was rubbing alcohol, over a cotton ball he held with forceps. He lit the cotton ball, then held it inside the jar for a few seconds. He dropped the forceps and placed the jar, top down, onto her back. He repeated this process with several more glass jars. I noticed her skin looked like it was being sucked up into the jars. "The heat creates a vacuum," James told me as I watched in awe as her skin continued to rise under the jar, then finally stopped. She lay like that for several minutes, then the man removed the jars from her skin, leaving large, red, raised circles all over her back.

I'd found the fire cupping demonstration to be a bit of a turn-on, despite my innate fear of fire and burns. It was quite exciting to watch how calm the woman was, just lying peacefully on the table, trusting completely that the man above her would hurt her in only the best of ways. It had been clear she enjoyed the act in an almost Zen-like fashion, and I envied the peaceful quality of both the participants and the fire cupping itself. It was quite different than the spankings and floggings James had administered to me. While I enjoyed those more than I expected I would, I wondered what something like this might feel like. Something, perhaps, *without* the fire. I just wasn't ready for that.

As we headed back to the bar for a second round of drinks, I noticed that the party goers were beginning to let loose and have fun. There was a woman securing a younger-looking guy to a St. Andrews Cross against the wall. Once she'd tied his wrists and ankles to the cross, she began flogging his chest, sides, and thighs. I noticed with interest that she seemed to really enjoy teasing him by letting the falls of the flogger almost caress the bulge at the front of his jeans, then she'd pull it back and strike him hard, making him yelp like a puppy that had been kicked. I laughed to myself, knowing my inner sadist would love that.

When we reached the bar, we stood next to a man who was with a diminutive girl who clearly enjoyed age play, one of the things I'd learned a lot about earlier that day in my research online. It was something that merely reading about made me cringe, and seeing it in person was an eye opener. He absentmindedly patted her hair as she played with a My Little Pony toy. Her pink ruffled skirt barely covered her ass, and I was horrified when I caught myself admiring how tight and firm it was. He asked her if she wanted a Coke, and she replied, "Yes, Daddy," and at that point I had to just look away. Everyone had their kink, but that was something I just wasn't prepared to see firsthand.

I was roused from my thoughts by another Long Island Iced Tea, which James handed me with a big smile. "Enjoy it, Kit, this is your last drink of the night." I made a fake pout, and he swatted my ass. "Don't be a baby, Kit, or I'll make you call me Daddy." He'd clearly seen me staring at the couple next to us, and he probably realized it had bothered me a bit. I rolled my eyes at him and sipped my drink. We walked around a bit more, and as we explored the party, James was sure to ask what I thought about each new form of play we encountered. I found the rope suspension demonstration interesting, but it certainly wasn't something I had the attention span to participate in myself. It was almost like performance art; very elegant, and it also had that Zen-like element that I appreciated, but it wasn't for me.

We stopped for a few moments to watch a woman and two men dripping melted wax all over the chest and stomach of a woman lying on a sheet of plastic. The flames gave me pause, but the woman didn't seem to be bothered a bit as the melted wax splashed on her flesh, then immediately congealed into interesting patterns. I nodded to James and smiled, and he seemed to make a mental note that I'd be open to giving that a try sometime. The next stop was a cutting demonstration. A woman was wielding a scalpel, making small, artful cuts on the lower back of her partner. We stood there long enough to see the last few strokes of the scalpel, and to watch her gently wipe away the blood with a towel. *"Slave"*, it said in large, red letters across his back. James caught me smiling as I watched, and he looked both perplexed and pleased.

"Well, this has been interesting and enlightening, but we have to head upstairs now," James said, taking my hand and pulling me away from the blood play scene. I hadn't realized there *was* an upstairs, and I was excited to see what else might be going on. My fetish experience had been limited to blindfolds and spankings, so this new world was more than a little bit fascinating. We made our way up the narrow stairwell into a smaller lounge area with ambient music playing softly in the background. There was another bar to our left, but it didn't appear to be staffed. A couple sat on a small velvet loveseat in the corner; they were whispering to each other and didn't seem to even notice we were there.

I looked around, disappointed that there didn't appear to be anything interesting going on after all. Just as I began to ask if we could go back downstairs, a man appeared, holding a large silver case. "Robert! So glad you made it," James said, shaking the man's hand enthusiastically. "Robert, this is my submissive, Kit." I was taken aback by his words; I had never been introduced in such a manner. I noticed the look of sheer joy on James' face, and I realized that he was *proud* to show me off. A week ago I may have been offended by this, but tonight it made me feel loved and appreciated. I smiled and greeted Robert warmly.

"So, are we ready for this?" Robert said, looking at James. James nodded and took my hand, leading me to the far corner of the lounge, where there was another massage table set up. I looked questioningly at James, not quite sure what was happening.

"Remember the violet wand site you showed me online?" he asked, and I nodded. "My dear friend Robert has the best violet wand kit money can buy, and he was generous enough to meet up with us so he could show you how it works, in person." My initial reservations faded as I watched Robert pop open his large metal case, revealing a violet wand and a huge assortment of attachments. I'd seen many of them online, but some were completely foreign to me. I'd enjoyed watching the videos online of the wand in use, and I'd been so curious about what it felt like, and whether or not I could handle something that looked pretty impressive and daunting in the photos and videos.

Robert pulled out a large glass bulb adapter and screwed it into the wand. He plugged the wand in to a foot pedal, and plugged the pedal's cord into the wall outlet next to the table. "Hop on up there, Kit," Robert said casually, and I shrugged and sat on the table. Robert laughed and shrugged. *Was I supposed to lie down?* I remained seated, and Robert tapped the pedal, which made the glass bulb glow a pretty purple, like a tiny plasma ball. It made a faint buzzing sound, and the sound increased as he turned the dial. He held the wand out and ran the bulb along his forearm. Tiny sparks leapt from the bulb to his arm, making zapping sounds as he moved the wand.

I jumped a bit at the sight of it, feeling suddenly quite anxious about being touched with the wand. Had I *really* wanted to try this out? Watching the videos had been fun, and I'd quietly hoped to maybe see one being used on someone *else* at the party tonight. I hadn't planned on being the recipient! Robert noticed my trepidation. "No worries, Kit," he said reassuringly, "this is the gentlest attachment, and if anything, it tickles. It's got *way* more bark than bite." I took a deep breath and hoped I'd agree.

I held my arm out, and as the wand moved toward me, I felt my heart begin to race. The bulb got close enough to my skin that sparks began to shoot out and make contact with my skin, and I jumped a bit, just from the surprise of a new sensation. As the wand travelled up my arm, I realized Robert had been right; it felt like bubbles on my skin than like shocks of electricity, and I enjoyed watching the purple glow of the bulb and the bright sparks emanating from it. As he brought the wand up my arm, it tickled more, and I laughed. Robert pulled the wand away and looked at me sternly. "You think this is funny, huh?" He turned the dial at the base of the wand, and the buzzing sound grew louder. He touched it to his arm, nodded, then put the wand close to my forearm. I jumped again, this time because it felt more like tiny stings than tickles. It didn't quite hurt, but it was definitely more intense.

James was suddenly at my side, and he put his arm around my shoulder. "Time to lie on your stomach, Kit," he said softly. I looked at him with an expression of silent protest, but he shook his head. "Nope, you're not getting out of this. Lie down." I begrudgingly turned over and lay down on my stomach, turning my head to the left so I could still see Robert and the wand.

72

Robert returned to his toy box, removed the large bulb from the wand, and replaced it with a glass electrode that looked more like a small spoon. I'd read about this one online; apparently it had more concentrated power than the larger bulb. *Uh-oh.* He switched the wand back on, tested it out on his arm, and turned the dial a bit. As he got closer, I could no longer see exactly what he was doing, but I felt the electrode make contact with my shoulder. I made a sound that resembled a dog chewing on a squeak toy, and I immediately felt James' hand on my other shoulder, gently rubbing my skin as if to comfort me. Being simultaneously tortured and soothed; well, *that* was new.

The wand trailed from my shoulder to the top of my corset, then back up, to my neck. I flinched a bit at first, the sparks causing a much sharper sensation on the sensitive skin of my back. I smiled to myself as I realized I was somehow getting used to the sensations, and even beginning to enjoy them. Just as I settled in to the feeling and rhythm of it, Robert switched the wand off and returned to his box of attachments. James followed him, and they quietly discussed which one to use next. James reached for one, and Robert handed the wand to him.

A surge of excitement ran through me as I realized James would wield the wand this go-round. As he approached, I saw that the new attachment was an even smaller glass electrode, and I knew that meant it would hurt more than the last one. I was ready. I was almost anxious for it, I wanted to feel it, to see if I could handle it, to see if my body would adapt quickly, as it had with the last one.

James tapped the foot pedal, and the now-familiar buzzing sound filled the air around me and gave me goose bumps. I closed my eyes this time, just waiting for the new sensation. Expecting it on my back, I jumped when it instead touched my upper thighs. I flinched so hard I thought I'd fall off the table, and James laughed. "Well, now I know what gets your attention," he said, then he brought the wand up to my shoulder and followed the same path along my skin that Robert had, this time making several more tracks along the same route. It hurt considerably more than the spoon-shaped attachment, but it quickly began to feel quite good, and I caught myself moaning softly as the sparks danced along my skin.

I felt James' hand pulling the strings of my corset as he continued to glide the wand back and forth, then he yanked the corset down until it was practically around my hips. My brief concerns about being exposed in front of Robert or anyone else who might pass by faded quickly as he turned the intensity of the wand higher and began to make

74

long vertical paths with it, from my neck almost down to my waist, then back up again. I gasped a bit from the feel of it on the tender flesh near my waist, but it still somehow felt good.

James continued moving the wand over me for several minutes, then he switched it off and gently glided his hand across my back. "Can you handle any more, Kit?" He asked me. I nodded, finding myself rather unable to form words. "Good," he replied as he walked back to the box and pulled out an attachment which looked to be made entirely of metal. Not even a little bit scared by this point, I simply closed my eyes and relaxed into the cushioned table, ready for the next round.

I heard the telltale buzzing sound and felt James standing near me. He passed his hand over my back, rubbing my shoulders, then the middle of my back, then along my waist. His hand felt cool and soft, but I was ready for the sting of the wand. When he gave it to me, I let out a yell; the metal attachment had a lot more *bite* than *bark,* and it hurt like hell. He lowered the intensity, then began passing it across my skin, and while it was much more intense than the glass had been, the sharp pain worked its way into a rhythm, and I found myself beginning to enjoy this one as well.

Each time he brought it closer to my waist, I jumped, and soon he kept the strokes of the wand higher up, sticking with my shoulders and upper back. He turned the dial a bit, making the pain even sharper, but this time I didn't scream. I tried my hardest to stay still, to not scream, but I realized I was tensing my muscles up quite tightly in my efforts to remain still and quiet. "It's okay," he leaned in and whispered. "No one else is up here. Make noise if you need to." With that, he turned the dial up again, and I let loose, grasping the sides of the table and crying out as wave after wave of intense, burning pain hit me. He continued on despite my screams, making even, constant passes up and down my skin.

The burning sensation became so severe I was sure I couldn't bear another second. *Hadn't burning been my one big no-no?* I thought to myself through my screams, but at the same time something in me refused to yell out my safe word, which I knew would immediately end this experience. I was aware that I could make it stop at any time, but something in me wouldn't let me do it. Part of it was my inability to admit failure, but a big part of it was my desire to see how far I could go, how much I could really endure.

James cranked the dial up yet again, and I literally saw stars. I clenched my eyes tightly, grasped the sides of the table as if I thought the pain might send me flying across the room, and let out a shriek that an hour before would have embarrassed me to no end. Not now, though. I didn't care who was there, who saw me, who heard me. I was in my own world, a world of pain and amazing new feelings I'd never experienced. James made long strokes across my back with the wand, and I began to breathe in the smell of burning flesh. My worst fear, but somehow it didn't even faze me. I wanted more pain, more burning, more *everything*. And that's exactly what I got.

He turned it up just a bit more, and I thought I'd black out. I felt nothing but one line of burning flesh after another, over and over and over again, and I suddenly realized I was screaming and thrashing around on the table like a lunatic. James' hand rested on my shoulder, as if to keep me from falling off the side, and he continued at his work, making large zigzags across my skin. Just as I knew I couldn't take one more second of the wand, I felt a sort of numbness take over me, and the pain faded, bit by bit, until suddenly it felt like I was hardly being touched. The stinging metal attachment felt as though it had stopped torturing me and was now lovingly caressing me, causing me to moan softly as my body went completely limp.

I don't even know how much time passed. I didn't hear the music anymore, and while I knew James was standing there touching me, I could hardly perceive what sensation was his hand and what was the wand. I felt like I was floating, like any pain I'd ever had was gone, like all was as right with the world as it could ever be. My mind felt emptier than it had ever felt. I wasn't thinking about work, about people staring at me, about how I looked, lying there half naked on a massage table. I wasn't thinking about a single thing, except for how lovely I felt in that moment.

I felt like I could fall asleep right there, but I didn't want to miss out on that feeling; I didn't want it to stop. I realized the wand was gone, and that James was leaning over me, kissing the back of my head, running his fingers through my hair, massaging my back. It felt muffled, like I was experiencing the world through a soft focus filter. I hardly knew my own name; all I knew was soft, cushiony bliss. I lay there, enjoying that warm, glistening softness, until I began to come to, to slowly feel more aware of what was happening around me.

The music was louder, and more people had filtered into the lounge. I opened my eyes and saw groups of people crowded around the now-open upstairs bar. Everyone seemed to be engrossed in their various conversations, and not a single one was looking in my direction. James was crouched down next to me, his face at the same level as mine. "You okay, Kit?" he asked sweetly, still touching my hair. I nodded and smiled stupidly, and he smiled back. "Let's get you to that loveseat over there before someone else takes it." I nodded again but made no effort to move. He smiled at me again, then stood up and took my hand, helping me off the table. I lost my balance and nearly careened into a couple standing nearby, but James caught me, put one arm around my shoulder and one around my waist, and we walked to the red velvet loveseat against the wall.

I practically collapsed into it, and James walked quickly to the bar, retrieved a cup of ice water, and brought it to me. He held it up as I sipped, as though I was a complete invalid, but it didn't bother me; I appreciated his help. I didn't feel motivated to move, to lift my arms, to do *anything*. Once I'd finished the cup of water, I lay down on James' lap, enjoying the feeling of his hands gently caressing me as I watched the crowd moving about the room. Some were talking, some were dancing, and a few were making out. Robert seemed to have left. I took a deep breath and closed my eyes.

I felt James lifting me off his lap, and when I opened my eyes, the lounge appeared to have cleared out. Only a few people remained, and most of them looked quite intoxicated. *How long had I been lying there?* "Ready to go, Sleepyhead?" James said, and I laughed, rubbed my eyes, and nodded. I felt somewhat back to my normal self, and it suddenly occurred to me that my back felt like a huge slab of tenderized meat. I winced as I stood up, and as my corset began to fall I grabbed it quickly and yanked it back up. James pulled the strings just tight enough to keep the corset up, but not so tight that I'd end up screaming out in pain as it closed in around my raw flesh. Still, with each step I took, I felt like I might cry. It was as if someone had poured gasoline all over me and lit a match. I silently hoped I'd make it to the car without passing out.

Fortunately, the car was right outside the front door, and I sank into the seat, closing my eyes and breathing as evenly as I could, telling myself I wouldn't cry any more. James helped me buckle in, then he leaned over and kissed me on the cheek. "I'm sorry if I took that too far, Kit. You seemed to be enjoying it, and I wanted to see if we could get you to fly." *Fly. Yeah, That's what I'd done. And it was amazing. And it was worth this pain. I think.* I leaned over and kissed him on the mouth, moaning from the soreness all over my body as I pressed my lips against his.

"All good," I muttered unconvincingly as I put my hand in his. James drove us home and helped me into the house and out of my clothes. He grabbed the bottle of aloe and again rubbed it, very carefully, all over my back and shoulders. The lotion felt cool and wonderful, but the burning was still present, and I wondered how I'd sleep. As I pondered that thought, I must have fallen asleep in spite of my fears, because I woke up around seven the next morning, lying in that same spot, still on my stomach. *Shit,* I thought. *I never took my makeup off or brushed my teeth!* I hopped up and ran into the bathroom to remedy that, and as I stood at the mirror with my toothbrush in hand, I turned around and looked back at the mirror, to see if I had any marks from the night before.

Jesus Christ. My back was covered with what appeared to be hundreds of dark red lines, many of which were raised and angry looking. As horrific as it looked, it made me smile. *I'm more of a badass than I thought!* I brushed my teeth and washed my face, then realized with a start that today was shopping day. Which meant trying on

81

clothes with Marissa. *Shit*. Sure, I'd planned to fill her in on the exciting details of the past few days, but I'd intended on giving her the edited version that she was more likely to understand, to be cool with. Ah well, I realized I'd better avoid trying on any clothes with her if there was any chance of that working out.

I climbed back into bed, where James was still slumbering peacefully. It occurred to me that we hadn't even had sex last night, and a wave of guilt overcame me. He'd done so much for me, and I'd passed out on him. I think he realized how spent I was by the time we got home, but I still felt bad. I lay there, watching him sleep, and I must have drifted off again, because when I opened my eyes it was nine o'clock, and James was awake and looking at *me*. Relieved that I'd gotten up and brushed my teeth earlier, I scooted closer to him and slipped my hands behind his neck, pulling him in and kissing him deeply. His arms found my back and grabbed me hard, and I gasped into his mouth as the burning pain sunk deep into my flesh.

He seemed to enjoy this, and he dragged his hands across my back, scratching my raw skin until tears streamed down my face. I leaned back and half-glared at him, not sure I was up for more pain at the moment. He smiled and released his grip on my tattered back; instead, his hands found my cunt, and his finding it surprisingly wet, he plunged two fingers into me. I closed my eyes and sighed; as much as I'd enjoyed the previous night's festivities, I had other needs right now, and I was thrilled that he wanted to fulfill them. After kissing me deeply, James said, "I think I owe you something from yesterday. You fell asleep before I could give it to you."

He continued working his fingers inside me, and I threw my head back and moaned loudly. It normally took a little more than that for me to get worked up, but my nerve endings seemed to be on high alert. My body still felt like it was humming with energy, and I was responding to his hand in an incredible way. I could feel the tension building up, and when he brought his other hand closer and rubbed my clit with his thumb, I thought I'd explode. I remembered the other night, when he'd kept me from coming, and I took a few deep breaths until the approaching orgasm subsided. My body continued to pulsate, to vibrate under his touch, as he slid his thumb across the slick surface of my clit and thrust his fingers into my pussy, rubbing that perfect, rapidly swelling spot with each stroke.

My breathing became jagged, rough, and moans began escaping my mouth, louder and louder. Finally, the pressure built up past the point of no return, and I cried out, my entire body convulsing violently as I came. He continued working me over, and my body continued shaking, coming, again and again until I could take no more. I grasped his hand to push it away, but he continued stroking me, thrusting into me, slower now, as I relaxed back into the bed. He smiled at me, knowing I was usually very much *done* with being touched after coming so hard. *He* wasn't finshed just yet, though, and he wasn't going to allow me to be finished either.

I reached out for his cock, wanting to stroke it as he touched me, but he slapped my hand away, then he slid down until his head was between my legs and began to lap gently at my cunt. My clit was so swollen it felt like it would burst, and each time his tongue passed over it, it was amazing, so intense I almost couldn't take it. His tongue continued working my clit slowly and softly, and again he plunged his fingers into me, this time more forcefully. Once more, that pressure, that gorgeous tension, built up inside me, warming me and making my muscles contract again and again.

I held out for as long as I could, then once again screamed out as I came harder than anything I'd ever experienced. It was almost like the night before; in that brief moment, everything else went away, and there was only pleasure, but this time instead of lying quietly, my body convulsed, and I was unable to stop writhing fiercely, almost falling over the side of the bed, onto the floor. James caught me and held me tight as the shaking slowed and stopped, and as I lay there panting and sweating.

Before I could fully catch my breath, James was on top of me, pushing his cock into me roughly, grunting with each violent thrust. I winced and cried out as the raw flesh of my back was pressed into the bed, but he continued plunging into me so forcefully that I thought he'd push me through the mattress. My cunt was so sensitive that each thrust nearly sent me over the edge again, and it began to contract around his cock as another orgasm approached. He took this as a cue to fuck me even harder, and he growled loudly as his cock rammed into me. It was raw, animalistic, and hotter than hell. He'd exercised so much control the night before, with the wand, making sure to give me just what I needed to get me where he wanted me to be; now was his turn to let go, to let his inner beast take over.

And take over it did. He grasped my throat roughly, squeezing just enough that I couldn't breathe. My gasping for breath seemed to turn him on, and he pressed a bit harder, then grabbed my hair with his other hand and yanked my head back until I screamed. His eyes looked wild, feral, completely devoid of any self-control. He released his grip on my throat, replacing his hand with his mouth, biting my shoulders and my neck, a low growl emanating from him as he tore into my flesh with his teeth. He continued pounding into me as he bit me, again and again, until I was sobbing. And I loved every minute of it.

James came with a loud grunt and collapsed on top of me, completely spent. I enjoyed his weight bearing down on me, pinning me, I enjoyed reveling in the fresh, new pain mingled with the throbbing, stinging pain in my back from the night before. He lay there on top of me for quite some time, until I thought he'd fallen asleep, but then he slid off of me and lay to my left side. He looked at me, almost with awe in his eyes, and I wanted so badly to know what he was thinking, to ask him what was going through his mind. Not wanting to ruin the moment, I remained still and quiet. He kissed me very gently, barely grazing my lips with his own, and he ran his fingers up and down the side of my face, so softly I almost couldn't feel it. He looked so serene, so peaceful, so *content*. And I realized that even though my body felt like it was on fire, I felt quite content myself. Moreso than I could have ever imagined.

James finally gave me one more kiss, then he headed for the shower. I glanced at the clock and realized I'd better do the same too, or I'd be late for my shopping date with Marissa. I lay there until he finished his shower, and my mind was swirling with thoughts of him, of us, of the past twelve hours and how amazing it had all been. I felt a hint of sadness knowing that this wonderful holiday weekend was coming to a close, that "real life" had to resume all too soon. I found myself running my fingers along the collar around my neck, enjoying the feel of the leather, and of the steel ring at the front. I smiled to myself, wondering what Marissa would think of it if I decided to leave it on. To my chagrin, James entered the bedroom and noticed me lying in bed touching my collar, and he had a different idea. "Go ahead and take it off until tonight," he said nonchalantly. "Enjoy your shopping trip, we'll continue where we left off when you get back." *Hmph.*

I got out of bed, unbuckled the collar and handed it to him, and he grabbed me and kissed me. He gave me a slight swat on the ass as I walked to the shower, and I realized that was the one area that *didn't* hurt like hell. I smiled, wondering if he might do something to change that later that night. As I stepped into the shower, the full extent of the violet wand's effect hit me. The water felt like molten lava streaming down my back, and I turned around quickly for fear I'd pass out right there in the shower. I showered as fast as humanly possible, realizing that while I'd enjoyed receiving the pain, and even enjoyed feeling it as I lay in bed, *this* was not remotely enjoyable. It was pure misery.

When I stepped out of the shower, James was just walking into the bathroom to brush his teeth. He caught a glimpse of my back and his eyes widened. "Need some more aloe, Kit?" he asked, looking quite concerned. Without waiting for an answer, he retrieved the bottle, helped dry me off, and gently applied lotion all over my shoulders and back. My skin felt better almost instantly, but I knew that was only temporary. I was *not* looking forward to trying on clothes at the mall.

After I dressed and brushed my teeth, I found James sitting on the sofa, absent-mindedly messing around on his laptop. When I sat down next to him, he set the computer aside and put his arm around me, carefully avoiding my various bruised and burned spots. His expression was serious, and I was worried I'd done something wrong.

"Your collar is off, so right now you're not my sub, you're just my girlfriend. I need to know if I've gone too far, if I've scared you or hurt you too much." He looked away as he awaited my reply, as if he was certain I'd unleash a torrent of complaints and criticisms. Instead, I threw my arms around him and hugged him tightly, then took his face in my hands, forcing him to look me in the eyes. When he realized I was smiling, his eyes lit up, and I almost thought he'd cry.

"No, James," I answered, "It's been the best two days of my life. I can't even explain how much I have loved this. Even when I kind of hate it, I love it. Does that make sense?" James smiled back at me and nodded.

"Perfect sense. God, Kit, you're amazing. Thank you." He kissed me softly, and once again with more passion, more urgency, then he pulled back. "I know you need to get going. I can't wait to see you tonight, Kit. Really." I gave him one more quick kiss, then I looked at him again, making sure there was no trace of concern left on his face.

"I can't wait to put my collar back on," I said with a smile, and with that, I left to meet Marissa.

Chapter Eight

By the time I arrived at the mall, Marissa was already waiting for me. She rolled her eyes as she saw me approaching, and I stuck my tongue out at her. She knew I was always a little late, and she needed to get over it. "I thought I'd die of hunger waiting for you, Kit," she complained with an exaggerated sigh. "Wanna hit P.F. Chang's before we shop?" Well, I didn't particularly care for the place, but I knew it was her favorite, and they *did* have pretty good scallops, which was rather unheard of for a mall restaurant. I nodded in begrudging assent, and we made our way there.

As we passed the pet shop, I paused to look at a cage sitting right at the entrance. It was practically overflowing with tiny black kittens, and I thought I'd cry. I'd wanted a kitten for so long, but James was strictly anti-feline. I'd had a cat when I was a teenager, but it had been hit by a car, and I'd never fully gotten over it. I felt a tear welling up in my right eye, and I quickly blinked it away. I didn't want to endure hours of ridicule by hard-hearted Marissa, who thought animals were good for pretty much three things: breakfast, lunch, and dinner. I shook off my daydreams of taking home a little cat, knowing it just wasn't going to happen, and we continued on to the restaurant.

Once we'd gotten seated and ordered our food, Marissa began giving me the evil eye. "What's your deal, Mar?" I asked, wondering why she was staring at me so intently.

"Something's up with you, Kit, and I know it, so you better go ahead and just tell me now, so we don't have to talk and shop at the same time. You know how that fucks with my sale-finding mojo." I laughed, knowing all too well what a serious shopper she was, and how she hated shopping alone, but she also hated being distracted in any way when she was on the prowl for a deal. I'd known Marissa for ten years, and she'd been that way since we met. It was endearing, in a twisted sort of way. I laughed to myself, thinking about the degree to which *twisted* seemed to be the theme of my life these days.

"*See?* What's with the face, and the laughing? Fess up, what's going on? Are you having an affair or something?" I nearly choked on my water, wondering how in the hell she'd come up with such an absurd scenario. "I'm kidding, Dumbass," she quickly added. "Just tell me what's going on, because I can tell I'm missing something juicy. And for the love of God, I could use some juicy gossip right now."

Marissa had broken up with her boyfriend a few months back, and for reasons I couldn't quite comprehend, she was having trouble with the dating scene. I'd tried repeatedly to help her get a date, but nothing ever seemed to pan out. I wasn't sure if she was being overly picky, or if we were just happening upon an unusually high ratio of douchebags. Either way, things hadn't been so great for her lately, and I knew she was miserable, cranky, and sexually frustrated, to put it mildly.

I paused for a moment, trying to figure out exactly what to tell her; she'd always enjoyed hearing tales of my various sexual adventures, but this was a bit different, and I wasn't certain of how she'd react. I took a deep breath and decided to just lay it all out there. "Well," I began, "James and I are, uh, experimenting with some Dom/sub stuff." Before I could continue, her eyes widened and she interrupted me.

"Cool! Like role-playing? Like Nine and a Half Weeks? Or more like Story of O? Are you the one doing the dominating, or is he?" I smiled, relieved that she didn't seem to be the least bit troubled by what I thought might be a shocking revelation of some kind.

"Well," I went on, "Not really like either of those books. We're kind of doing it our own way. And he's the Dominant one, as shocking as you may find that." Marissa laughed, knowing what a domineering nutjob I could be from time to time; well, *most* of the time.

"Ha!" She said. "Good for James. Somebody needs to put you in your place." *Wow*, I thought. *She's really got me pegged.* I'd worried the whole drive to the mall that I'd be getting a lecture about letting a man boss me around, take advantage of me, tell me what to do. Apparently, Marissa had already determined I was desperately in *need* of someone to do just that.

As we enjoyed our lunch, we played fifty questions, with Marissa asking me pretty much everything under the sun about the few days I'd been experimenting with being a submissive. Never one to shy away from personal questions, we ended up discussing how sex had been different and what sorts of kinky play we'd tried out. She was so engrossed in listening to the details that she practically forgot to eat. I had to remind her several times to finish her food as I gave her a vivid accounting of all the fun I'd experienced, and how excited I was about it. Marissa was veritably beaming by the end of lunch, and I found that rather puzzling. Of course, she hadn't gotten

94

laid in months, so living vicariously through me, or anyone else, was probably fun for her. And something a bit out of the ordinary just made it all the more interesting.

We finished our lunch and entered the shopping phase of our day, during which time all talk of sex and beatings and submission ceased. Finding a good deal was serious business, and Marissa couldn't let her perverse interest in the details of my sex life sidetrack her. She was a woman on a mission. That mission lasted four painful, dismal hours, but I was the ever-faithful friend, holding her bags as she tried on dozens of outfits carefully selected from the clearance racks of store after store. I laughed to myself, thinking that she apparently had a little bit of Dominant in her too. She certainly had no problem bossing me around, in the friendliest of ways, if that meant she could shop, try on, and purchase more efficiently.

I was able to grab a few outfits along the way myself, and I was pretty pleased with my purchases. I stuck with things I knew would fit, hoping to spare my sore back the trauma of trying things on. By the time Marissa maxed out her credit card, I was exhausted and very much relieved to escape the clutches of the mall. We walked to the parking garage, and Marissa hugged me, laughing as I winced. "Got some bruises, huh?" She said with a smirk. "You kinky kids have fun. And *do* keep me updated. God knows I need the distraction." I told her I'd email her during the week, and we walked to our respective cars.

By the time I got home, I was physically and mentally frazzled. I kissed James on the cheek, told him my day had gone surprisingly well, tossed my bags on the floor of the bedroom, and literally fell into the bed and passed out. I napped for hours, having disturbing dreams of falling, of being lost, of having a final exam for a class I hadn't even registered for. I woke up feeling even more exhausted, and I mocked myself for my overly obvious symbolic dreams. Did I really feel that out of my depth in all this? My conscious mind was reveling in the newness, the sense of fun that had been injected into my life and my relationship, and even the power dynamic that put me a few notches under my partner, at least part of the time. But clearly my subconscious had concerns about this new situation.

Fuck my subconscious, I thought to myself, angry that it had caused me such a restless nap and left me feeling as tired as I'd been before lying down. I got up, rubbing my eyes and yawning, and I went to find James, who was outside mowing the lawn. I sat on the front porch and watched him, enjoying the sight of him pushing the mower across the lawn with a look of complete agony. *I AM a bit of a sadist*, I thought, then my softer side kicked in and I went inside to grab him a bottle of cold water.

When I brought James the water, he stopped the mower long enough to open it and gulp it down in five seconds flat. He handed me the empty bottle and wiped the sweat from his forehead. "Will you be putting the collar back on tonight?" He asked, raising an eyebrow as he awaited my reply.

"Of course," I said. "I can't wait." He smiled and winked at me before starting the mower back up. *Did he really just do that? Cheeseball.* I rolled my eyes at him but forgave him the wink since he was busting his ass in the 102 degree heat to make sure the neighbors didn't come knocking on our front door to bitch about how high the grass had gotten. I went back inside, decided to suffer through another shower so I'd be squeaky clean for whatever fun the night held, then I hopped back online to indulge my OCD need to read a bit more on all things BDSM. The more I read, the more I realized that these few days of fun and new experiences held the promise for something more, for us to grow as partners and as people. Sure, Marissa had enjoyed giggling about the role-play aspect of things; but there was much more to it, and I looked forward to exploring it all. With that, I put my collar back on and awaited whatever James had in store for me.

As I eagerly read, and read, and read, James sulked his way back into the house, exhausted from the arduous chore of grass-cutting in the July New Orleans heat. Noticing the collar was already around my neck, he immediately perked up. "Ah, my sub is back," he said with a tired smile. "I'm seriously craving some sesame seed cookies. Mowing the lawn sapped me, I need some carbs." Without another word, he disappeared into the bedroom, and I heard the shower running moments later. I sat there, not quite used to this aspect of our new, part time power differential. I shrugged to myself, then slipped on my flip flops, grabbed my purse and keys, and drove to Angelo Brocato's to procure a bag of fresh sesame seed cookies for my beloved Dominant.

I smiled to myself as I drove, feeling that little rush I'd grown quite familiar with over the past few days. But the rush was usually related to being beaten, or to sex, not to running an errand. Jesus, just fetching cookies was giving me a sick thrill. I decided there wasn't a damned thing wrong with that, and I found a spot a block up the street, walked to Brocato's, and bought a dozen sesame seed cookies. While there, I also bought some spumoni, knowing James loved that as well. We rarely indulged in dessert, so I hoped he would be pleased to have an extra treat in the freezer to enjoy later in the week.

By the time I made it back home, James was out of the shower and relaxing on the sofa with a book. I practically sprinted towards him, excited to present my offering. He took the two bags from me and peeked inside, and a huge smile spread across his face. *"Fresh cookies?* Good job, Kit! And spumoni? Nice." He knew I'd passed four or five grocery stores that carried the cookies in favor of getting them fresh from the source, and he was clearly impressed. I was absolutely thrilled. I took the spumoni from him and put it in the freezer, then returned to the sofa so sit next to him as he enjoyed his cookies. "Some milk would be great," he said with another smile, and I returned to the fridge to get him a glass of milk.

I realized that a week ago I'd have scoffed at his requests and told him to get his own damned milk, and I marveled a bit at my perspective shift, at how the smallest task suddenly seemed to take on a bigger meaning and bring smiles to both our faces. I brought him his milk and sat with him, just smiling and thinking about how very happy I was at that moment. Once he'd finished his second cookie and the glass of milk, he stood up and looked down at me. "Bedroom," he said sternly. "Now."

The reaction my body had to his tone was immediate and intense. A chill passed through me as I jumped up from the sofa and walked quickly to the bedroom, with James following closely behind. As soon as we reached the bed, he ordered me to undress, then grasped my wrists and pulled them behind me. "Stand there," he said before walking to the armoire and returning with the wrist cuffs. He slipped them onto my wrists and pulled me by the cuffs to the wall on the other side of our bed. I looked up and noticed two large eye hooks in the wall; they hadn't been there this morning. *James had clearly been busy while I was at the mall*, I thought excitedly.

James fastened a wrist cuff to each eye hook, and I stood facing the wall, my arms above my head, shoulder length apart. From the corner of my eye I saw him pull a suede flogger from the bag we'd brought home from the sex shop. He slapped it against his hand in a mock-menacing way, giving me a look that resembled that of a comic book villain plotting the destruction of the world. I wanted to laugh, but I was also aware of how raw my back was, and how much even the slightest of floggings would hurt. Best not to laugh, I decided, so I just smiled and looked down. James stood behind me, and I felt the soft suede falls of the flogger dance gently across my back. He wasn't striking me; in fact, it felt more like he was trying to tickle me. But it was wonderful, and soothing, and I whimpered softly from the sheer pleasure of dozens of strips of suede caressing my tender flesh.

James set the flogger down and picked up something else I couldn't quite see. "You're ass seems to have survived the weekend unscathed," he said with a smirk. "Can't have that. I need you to remember me while you're sitting at your desk tomorrow." With that, I felt a large paddle make violent contact with my left ass cheek. The force of it pushed me forward until my body was pressed firmly against the wall. Before I could even try to breathe, he struck me again, and when I let out an embarrassing yelp, I heard James moan. He was hurting me in a new way, and he was clearly loving it. He smacked me several more times then ran his hand across my ass. "You're gonna hate me tomorrow," he observed as he began to wield the paddle again, this time focusing on my right cheek.

I pressed my face against the wall and stopped trying to avoid crying out. The pain was just too intense, and there was no use trying to be quiet when I realized he was enjoying hearing me scream. In fact, the louder I screamed, the harder he struck me, until he finally stopped, released my wrists, and lay me down on the bed. "How was that?" He asked, still making that evil villain face.

"Fucking awful," I replied in between jagged breaths.

"Did you like it?" He asked.

"I loved it," I said with an exhausted smile. He grabbed my legs and pulled me towards him, then he plunged his cock into me and fucked me forcefully until he came inside me with a loud moan.

Once we'd both recovered, we got up to complete our evening ritual of teeth-brushing and face-washing. As I brushed my teeth, James came up behind me and silently removed my collar. I felt a pang of loss sweep over me as the strip of leather was taken away, and I almost felt like I'd cry. Not wanting to ruin an amazing weekend, I kept my feelings to myself and focused on the fact that we'd have more wonderful weekends to come. We climbed into bed, and I fell asleep with James' arms wrapped lovingly around me.

Chapter Nine

Tuesday marked the beginning of a tragically long four-day work week. I found it difficult to concentrate, and I smiled to myself each time I shifted in my office chair, trying to find a way to comfortably sit with a welted ass. It made me feel alive, connected to James, desirous of more, and more, and *more*. And I got more, and then some, the following weekend, when James was waiting for me at the door Friday evening, collar in hand.

We continued on in this manner for months, my being regular girlfriend Kit most weekdays and submissive Kit on the weekends. Every once in a while James brought out the collar on a weeknight, and we'd have an unexpected several hours of pain and pleasure. I loved it when he did that, and on many workdays I sat at the office, trying to focus on some project or another while secretly hoping he'd be waiting at home with the collar in hand, ready to abuse me in some new way.

Marissa inquired often if the role-playing had gotten stale. She had no idea how deeply attached to my submissive side I was becoming, and how much my collared time with James meant to me. I sometimes wondered if *he* even knew. But we were having so much fun, and we were more in love than ever, and I felt I couldn't ask for much more than that. We went to parties some weekends where we got to see and try new types of play, and every time James came home with a bag or box, I just knew it was a new instrument of delicious torture, and I felt like a kid at Christmas. He treated me so well, and so sternly, and I loved it.

But I couldn't stop thinking about how little I wanted to be regular, plain, normal girlfriend Kit. Of course we had a great relationship even when that's all I was, but as the months passed, it began to feel empty somehow, as if I wasn't quite complete on those days which seemed to go on forever, without the promise of being abused, being put in my place, being told what to do and how to do it, and loving every moment of it. I mourned the loss of my submissive self, and I found myself anxiously awaiting her return, knowing that it was only then that I'd feel truly fulfilled.

Summer ended and fall was upon us, and as the days grew shorter, so did my patience with living as plain old Kit. We had a wonderful Thanksgiving holiday, during which James took full advantage of my weekend collared status by making Black Friday shopping lists for every damned store in the city. I shopped my bruised and welted ass off from midnight until noon, then returned home and passed out amidst dozens of shopping bags. James rewarded me with an early Christmas gift: my very own violet wand. I awoke from my long nap to find it wrapped and resting at the foot of the bed, and I was so happy (and delirious from twelve hours of shopping hell) that I burst into tears and cried for nearly half an hour.

He gave it a test run that night, and by Sunday night we had tried out every one of the ten attachments that came with the kit he'd purchased. My entire body was a patchwork of red dots, blotches, and lines, and I was convinced it was the best gift I'd ever received. It was also the best several days I'd had in a long while. I'd gotten to wear my collar from Wednesday evening until Sunday night, and when Sunday night finally arrived, I simply wasn't ready for it to end.

James was finishing up some work on his computer, so I got ready for bed alone, and instead of placing my collar on the top of his armoire, as I'd become accustomed to doing each Sunday night, I decided to leave it on. I'd never worn it to work before; in fact, I had a slight rush of panic as I considered the possibility that my coworkers may balk at the sight of my wearing a black leather collar with my

105

standard, conservative work attire. It was understated as far as collars went, but it nonetheless wasn't a typical workplace sight. I took a deep breath, also considering what James might think when he realized I was still wearing it the next morning. Would he think I'd simply forgotten to take it off? Would he notice it and remove it before I left? Suddenly filled with anticipation, I got into bed and pulled the covers up around me.

I fell asleep before James finished his work, and when I woke up the next morning he was fast asleep beside me. I got up, ate a quick breakfast, and began my very brief morning routine of getting ready for work. I threw on some clothes, brushed my teeth, and put on a little powder and eyeliner, acutely aware all the while that the collar was still buckled snugly around my throat. Just as I was about to run out the door, James woke up, and he stumbled into the bathroom, bleary eyed from a late night of unexpected work. He regarded me briefly, but there was little expression on his face other than utter fatigue. I hugged him and kissed him, and with that I was out the door and on my way to work.

I felt a buzz of excitement as I drove, as if I'd gotten away with something, as if I had somehow discovered a way to keep my "secret identity" even though it was time to get back to my normal workweek routine. I wondered if James had even noticed, or if he'd be shocked to see me walk through the front door later that evening, collar around my neck. Hell, I wasn't even certain I'd make it through the workday without feeling self-conscious and removing it before too many people saw me. *No, I resolved, I was keeping it on no matter what.* I smiled to myself, satisfied with my sudden steadfastness, and by the time I made it to work I felt quite confident that I'd go through my day without incident.

Much to my relief, my coworkers were so exhausted from a long weekend of family visits, shopping, and overeating that they'd have hardly noticed if I'd shown up to work sporting a third arm, much less a small leather band around my neck. No one paid any attention to me, and that unfortunately included my several emails to my staff requesting them to actually *turn in their work.* I didn't let it bother me, though, and by lunchtime I was already lost in thought about seeing James that night.

In the midst of my daydreaming, my phone beeped, and I picked it up to discover a text from him. *"Decided to be my sub at work, eh? Check your personal email. Now."* With a surge of anxiety, I minimized the spreadsheet I'd been working on and pulled up my email. The newest one

107

was from James, and the subject line read "Urgent Work Assignment." I opened it and quickly read it, and a lump formed in my throat. *"I couldn't help noticing your collar was still on this morning. I assume that was intentional? Either way, you're still mine right this very moment, and you're going to prove that to me. Click this link, you should find it rather…disturbing. I want you to masturbate while you watch it. I know you're in your cubicle and anyone may walk by. Figure it out. I expect a reply once you come, which you WILL DO. You have ten minutes. Go."*

James, being a professional computer geek, knew very well that our tiny office had no internet watchdogs, and that I was able to surf the web at will without anyone knowing what sites I visited. How did he know I wasn't in a meeting or something, though? I couldn't just drop everything I was doing to serve his every whim. I caught myself feeling a bit of resentment well up, and I quickly realized I was the one who'd made the choice to keep the collar on when I left for work. He'd noticed, and he was probably both pleased and shocked, and he was clearly testing me.

James obviously wanted to know if I really meant it. But Jesus, he'd asked a lot of me. It was noon, and much of the staff was at lunch, but several of the more work-obsessed staff always brought their lunch and ate in the office, not wanting to miss a precious moment of workday drudgery. I peeked outside my cubicle and looked around, seeing no one coming or going, and I clicked the link in the email. *Oh, for fuck's sake. It was Daddy/little girl porn.*

Now I understood that age play was as valid a kink as any, but it just *bothered* me, and James knew this all too well after I'd rambled on and on about it when we attended that first party. The site of the older man and *very* young woman acting like father and daughter at the bar had given me the creeps, and since then, whenever we personally witnessed any sort of age play, I just looked away. I certainly didn't judge them, but I had a visceral reaction to it that I just couldn't control. And here on my computer screen, to my utter dismay, was a young woman who must have been 21, but was dressed like a very young girl, holding a teddy bear and sucking on a lollipop. *This can't end well*, I thought, and I couldn't imagine even watching this video to the end, much less fondling myself to orgasm while doing so. In my cubicle. *At work.* What had I gotten myself into?

Yet in the midst of my horror at the video, and my anxiety at the thought of touching myself at my desk,

109

where any of my coworkers might walk by and catch me, I felt that familiar exhilaration in my chest that bubbled up whenever I did something for James, as his submissive. This was no different than driving across town to seek out his favorite exotic import beer at the drop of a hat, or stripping down and letting him flog me until I was a welted mess. I was being his sub, and I was doing it here, at work, and something about that felt quite marvelous.

I focused my attention on the video; the "little girl" was sitting in bed, hugging her teddy bear and sucking her lollipop. Of course, she was wearing a way-too-tight white button up shirt and an impossibly short plaid skirt. Her hair was in long blonde pigtails, and she wore white knee socks, but no shoes. An older man entered the room, looking angry, and slammed the door. Apparently the naughty girl had forgotten to do her chores, and he was *not* pleased with her. He slowly removed his belt, and the girl began to cry and beg him not to spank her.

It occurred to me suddenly that I was only fulfilling half of James' request. With a deep sigh and another few peeks up and down the row of cubicles, I nervously hiked my skirt up a bit, then slipped my right hand up my thigh and into my panties. I was shocked to find my pussy already wet, but I realized that the nervousness had surely caused it. It definitely wasn't the video, which was already making me feel positively queasy. I turned my chair towards the inner wall of the cubicle in an attempt for a slight amount of privacy and time to "recover" in case someone walked by.

To my utter shock, I found myself rubbing my clit enthusiastically, enjoying the feel of my hand on my pussy right there in the middle of my office. I knew James was sitting at work thinking about me masturbating for him, and that turned me on beyond belief. On my monitor, the girl was lying over the man's lap; he'd pulled her tiny skirt up and was beating her with his belt. Her white panties were soon yanked down so that he could spank her bare ass. She screamed and cried and begged him to stop, but he showed no mercy.

Watching the belt, then his hand, striking her ass until it was covered in welts sent a lightning bolt of pleasure to my cunt, and I felt aroused and ashamed all at once. The video was sick and twisted and wrong, but *God*, it was hot. I had almost forgotten where I was when I heard footsteps approaching my cubicle. I hastily pulled my skirt down and brought the spreadsheet back up, but when Paul poked his head in to bring me his report, he gave me a suspicious look. I was mortified, and I knew it was obvious I'd been up to *something*.

"What's going on, Kit?" Paul asked with a sly smile.

"Nothing, Paul, just finishing up my *employee reviews*." I hoped that little lie might shut him up.

"Ah, okay," he replied, "I thought maybe you were indulging in a little Cyber Monday shopping. That's okay if you are, it's *our little secret*." He handed me his report, gave me a knowing wink, and continued on his way. I sighed deeply, relieved that my coworkers were far too innocent to suspect I could be masturbating furiously to porn on my office computer, in the middle of the workday.

I shook off the minor interruption, then brought the video back up. It appeared that during our brief intermission, the man had had enough of spanking the girl's ass, and he'd moved on to forcing her to suck his sock. She was gagging and crying and saying, "Please Daddy, just fuck me." *Dear Lord.* And fuck her he did, after first tearing open her white shirt and exposing her small, very perky breasts. I felt a little more self-conscious, but again I slipped my hand under my skirt and began to touch myself.

As I watched him ram his cock mercilessly into her tight, pink cunt, I slipped a finger into my own pussy, thrusting in unison with his cock. He grabbed her hand and told her to be a good little girl and rub her clit, and as she complied, I slipped my finger out and rubbed my own. Just as she began to scream and moan, and he pulled out his cock and shot his load all over her chest and face, my entire body shook with a surprisingly powerful orgasm.

I closed out the video and sat there, completely stunned at what I'd just done, and at how easily I'd put my fears of being caught aside to do what I knew James wanted of me. I was quite relieved he'd sent the request during lunch when the office was mostly empty, and I wondered if that had been intentional, or just a lucky coincidence. After a quick trip to the ladies' room to make sure I didn't look completely disheveled, I sent James a text. *"Request completed, Daddy."* Within seconds, I received his reply.

"It wasn't a request, it was an order. And don't call me Daddy. It's gross." I laughed out loud, delighted that he always had a sense of humor, even when being my Dominant, then I smiled at the thought that he *was* being my Dominant today, on a Monday, in the middle of our workdays. It felt liberating in a way I couldn't even fathom, and I loved it.

Chapter Ten

The rest of the day flew by, as my afternoon was filled with meetings and a frenzy of emails regarding end-of-year tasks which must be completed before the Christmas holiday. Work was going to be getting a lot busier, and I figured that was probably a good thing. It definitely made the time pass more quickly, and it kept me from getting too lost in my thoughts. By five o'clock, though, I was ready to run out the door and get home to James. I texted him to let him know I was on my way home, and he replied immediately. *"I have a special surprise for you. Check email ASAP."* I tossed my bag back down and flipped my monitor back on, then opened up my email. There was an email right at the top from James, and it had no subject line. I opened it up, and it was simply a shopping list, most of which seemed to be for a pet we did not own. As I glanced over the list, I nearly squealed with excitement.

1. 14 inch collar, any color, with bell

2. Leash to match collar

3. Feather tipped cat toy

4. Water and food bowls

5. One pound bag of kitten food

6. Small litter box and bag of litter

Much to James' chagrin, I'd been asking, pleading, begging, and probably even *whining* for a kitten for years now. Each time, James would simply roll his eyes and tell me I was out of my damned mind. I nearly jumped up and down with delight at the thought of James coming home after work with a tiny furry bundle of joy for me to love. I wondered if my "bonus" day of submission had touched him to such an extent that he wanted to reward me. This seemed like a huge reward, given his distaste for anything with claws and whiskers, but then again, it had been such a phenomenal few months, perhaps he'd softened to the idea.

I snatched up my bag and my jacket, and I headed to the nearest pet store, a small boutique style shop that happened to be on the way home. The owner was very friendly, and she seemed pleased to have a new customer in her quiet shop. I explained the situation to her, and she was happy to help me purchase the items on my list. Knowing I'd want only the best for my new kitty, I spent far too long perusing the collars before settling on a thin black collar with tiny purple rhinestones and a little purple bell. Sure, it was a bit tacky, but it was just too cute to pass up. I gathered everything else, paid her, and rushed home to get everything perfect for the arrival of our new addition.

Time moved slowly, and by seven o'clock James still hadn't gotten home. I busied myself with some chores I'd been putting off for far too long, and I was rather pleased with myself for being so productive in the face of such anticipation. Around eight o'clock I heard the front door open and shut, and I ran excitedly into the foyer to greet James. I hugged him tight, practically jumping into his arms, but when I looked around for my new pet, it was nowhere to be seen.

"Go fill the food and water bowls, and put them in the bedroom," James instructed nonchalantly. I took care of it right away, smiling as I heard noises in the foyer and heard our bedroom door open and close. I practically bounded through the house, having to calm myself down lest I spill food and water all over the floor. I balanced the food bowl on my left arm so that I could open the bedroom door, and when it opened I nearly dropped both bowls right there in the doorway. There was no cat to be seen, but there was a young, attractive boy sitting next to James at the foot of the bed. Not sure what to think or do, I stood there, awkwardly holding a dish of cat food and a dish of water as the two of them stared silently at me.

"This is Michael," James finally said. "He happens to own the cutest little black kittens I've ever seen. He has one little girl who needs a home, but I'm just not totally convinced you're a cat person." I wrinkled my nose up as I looked at him, not quite sure how to respond. James continued on, "So I have a test for you. If you can play kitty for us and do a really good job, she's all yours." I looked down at the bowls in my hands, then at James, then at the boy. *Okay*, I thought, *this is not remotely what I was expecting.* "Put the bowls down on the floor," James instructed, "then get undressed." I had only one thought, which was suddenly caught on a repeating loop in my brain. *Was I being rewarded, or being punished, for wearing my collar today?*

With shaking hands, I carefully set the bowls down, certain that spilling their contents would mean no new pet for me. The lights in the bedroom were bright, and I felt rather self-conscious. Sure, I'd spent some time partially naked at parties the past few months while being beaten and otherwise abused, and honestly I hadn't cared much who saw what. Standing there naked, though, in front of this boy I'd never seen before was a rather daunting

117

proposition. I realized I had little choice in the matter, so I took a deep breath and quickly disrobed.

James picked up the rhinestone-encrusted collar I'd so carefully chosen, and he motioned for me to walk towards him. He removed my own collar and placed this one around my neck, buckled it tight, then fastened the leash to it. I felt rather silly, then when I noticed what was in his hands I realized I was about to feel even sillier. James stood up and attached a pair of red and black faux fur cat ears to my hair, and he smiled once he was satisfied that he had them placed just right.

"I don't know why I hadn't thought of this before, Kit. It's so fitting. Now get on your knees. Actually, get on all fours for us." Mortified and blushing, I dropped to the floor and got on my hands and knees. James picked up a black bag which had been sitting on the bed, and he retrieved from it a small bottle of lube and a black glass butt plug with a long, furry black tail. "This will be just perfect, Kitty," he said with a grin as he knelt behind me. He rubbed my ass gently then inserted a lubed up finger. I gasped, not because I was unfamiliar with the feel of his finger in my ass, but because I was unaccustomed to having someone stand over me, watching such an intimate act take place.

His finger was soon replaced by the cold, unyielding plug, and I jumped at the sensation. "There, there, Kitty, it's okay. Have some water; that will make you feel better." I looked back at James with widening eyes, and he motioned towards the water dish. Silently wishing for a hole to open up in my bedroom floor and swallow me up, I crawled forward towards the bowl and leaned down to lap up the water the best I could. Water splashed onto the carpet, and James slapped my ass hard. "Don't make a mess, Kitty. If one kitty makes a mess, we certainly can't have *two*."

I lowered my head to the bowl and very slowly licked at the water, careful not to spill a drop. I jumped as I felt something tickling my back, and I realized it was the feather toy I'd purchased. *Fuck, he's the devil!* I continued trying to drink water from the bowl as James tortured me with the feather, tickling me under the arms, on the thighs, and on the soles of my feet. I thought I'd pass out; I hated being tickled, and I usually flailed around like a lunatic at the slightest *hint* of it. It took every last bit of self-control to stay still and focus on the water bowl.

"Impressive, Kitty," James said, setting the tickler on the bed. He grabbed the end of the leash and tugged it towards him, forcing me up and away from the bowl. I knelt upright, but I kept my eyes cast downward; I couldn't bear to look at the boy next to James. I'd never felt so exposed, so humiliated, in all my life. James yanked the leash again, and I rose to my feet to stand before him. "Look at me," he said harshly, and I looked up and into his eyes. "Do you know what happens now?" I shook my head as thoughts raced through my mind of all the possibilities, all the sadistic plans he could have in store for me.

James smiled softly and slipped his hand under my chin, pulling me forward and kissing me. "What happens now is you go to the closet." Completely baffled, and worried about what awaited me when I returned, I walked through the bathroom and into our large walk-in closet. When I switched on the light, I looked down and found the tiniest black kitten I'd ever seen. She was sleeping in a small basket lined with a towel, but she opened her eyes, looked up at me, and let out a squeaky "meow" before stretching, climbing out of the basket, and standing at my feet.

I bent down, scooped up the precious kitten, and kissed the back of her neck. I could feel her purring, and for a moment I wasn't even aware of the fact that I was standing naked in my closet wearing kitten ears and a butt plug tail, while a stranger stood in my bedroom. That realization hit me soon enough, though, and I walked slowly back into the bedroom, wondering what might come next. To my surprise, the boy was nowhere to be seen, the lights had been turned down, and James was reclining in the bed, smiling at me.

I was more than a little stunned by the events of the evening, so I just stood there for a bit, petting the kitten absent-mindedly, until James asked me to get in bed with him. I lay on my side facing him, still holding the tiny cat, who seemed far too sleepy and content to leave my arms and explore her new home. I pulled the covers up over us, and James scooted closer to me and put his arm around me. "You really surprised me today, Kit," he began. "I noticed you wearing your collar this morning, and I didn't know what to think. I guess I wanted to see how much it meant. From what I can tell, it meant *a lot.*"

I nodded enthusiastically as James brushed my bangs out of my eyes, then he kissed my forehead softly. "I've enjoyed these past few months more than you know," he continued. "I've felt like I wanted more of you, but I didn't know if you wanted to *give* me more. I think maybe you do." Again, I nodded, feeling strangely speechless, for once. "Tell me, Kit," he said, looking terribly serious. "Do

121

you want to make this full time, and not just a weekend thing? Do you want to be completely mine, every day, even when it's hard, and not fun at all, to do what I ask of you?" Tears instantly flooded my face, and I could hardly form words. I was able to get out a barely audible "yes" in between sobs, but that was all that he needed of me.

"Good, then," James said with a tone of resolve in his voice. "I have a little bit of work to finish up. Take care of your cat and get ready for bed." With that, he wiped the tears from my face, kissed me quickly, and left the room. I *knew* I wanted to be truly his, and that this part-time arrangement was no longer enough for me. I was glad he felt the same way. I believed in my heart that I could handle whatever James had in store for me, and I wanted desperately to prove that to him. I cleaned myself up, set up the litter box, and got ready for bed. I crawled into bed and snuggled with my new kitten, not even realizing I was still wearing the collar I'd purchased for *her*.

The bedroom door opened, and James walked back in. He had a strange expression on his face, and I wondered what it meant. "Get up," he said, and as warm and cozy as I was, under the covers with my kitty, I got up, set her back down and covered her up, and stood beside the bed. James motioned for me to walk towards him. I stood in front of him, a curious smile creeping across my face. But James wasn't smiling; in fact, he looked *very* serious. I hoped I hadn't inadvertently done something wrong.

"On your knees," he ordered for the second time that night. Relieved, I immediately dropped to my knees and looked up at him. He bent down just enough to reach around to the back of my neck and unfasten the cat collar. I suddenly felt rather silly for leaving it on. He tossed it onto the bed, then he slid his fingers under my chin and pulled my head up, until I was again looking up at him. "Are you sure about this? That you want to be mine full time? Completely?"

"Yes," I replied. "More than anything."

"Get up," he said, holding my hand to help me back to my feet. He reached into his pocket and produced a thick silver bracelet. He opened it up, and I noticed that it had a hinge on one side, but I didn't see a clasp on the other. "Hold out your left arm," he instructed, and I did as he asked. He placed the bracelet on me, closed it around my wrist, then pulled a tiny bag from his pocket. It contained the tiniest screw I'd ever seen, and a tool designed just for it. James placed the screw in the small hole in the bracelet, and he tightened it until it was just about invisible. He returned the little wrench to his pocket before taking me by my shoulders and kissing my forehead.

"You never have to take this off," he said gently. "And no one but us has to know what it means." I found myself crying once again; *what a sap I'd become*. But I felt so emotional and so ecstatic that I couldn't help myself. I was his, body, mind and spirit, every minute of every day. I knew this new phase of our relationship would bring more challenges than I could anticipate, but I was ready for them. And I'd never be plain old girlfriend Kit again.

"So, are you ready to show me again how much you really want this?" James asked with a smirk. I nodded and smiled. *Oh yes, I certainly was.*

The Submissive Diaries Book Two

Sam's Assignments

By

Audra Morgan

The Submissive Diaries Two: Sam's Assignments

Copyright © 2013 by Audra Morgan

Audra can be contacted by email at

AudraMorganBooks@gmail.com

Prologue

My name is Sam, and I'm a submissive. I'm also a bit of a smartass, so don't go picturing some quivering, quiet wallflower lurking in the corner awaiting orders. It doesn't work like that for us. And he likes it that way. My Dom means the world to me, and there's *very* little I wouldn't do for him, or let him do *to* me. Unfortunately, he's been working on a special project at the office lately, and we just haven't had much time together. I just received an email from him, though, and I have a feeling he intends to keep me busy while he's stuck at work...

Dearest Sam,

I know how bored and lonely you get when I have to work long hours. I've arranged for some...diversions...to keep you occupied until my return. You will receive further details via text and email. Check both regularly. I expect full and immediate cooperation, and I want you to journal your experiences for my reading enjoyment.

Steven

I'm excited about the prospect of having some fun while Steven's away, but I'm also a bit terrified. Steven is not your typical Dominant; he doesn't flog me or tie me up or even really spank me on a regular basis. But he's a sadist. Boy, is he ever a sadist. He simply prefers other, more insidious methods of torture. Mind-fuckery is his specialty. And I have a feeling my mind will be well-fucked by the time his project at work comes to an end. The good news is that I'm a bit of a masochist myself, and I'll take my torture however he serves it up. I'm game for anything. *I think.*

Assignment One

"Come on, Steven, tell me *something*," I implored as I finished my makeup and walked into the closet to find something to wear. Sure, I've gotten better over the years with not having to know every last detail, but this was ridiculous. I'd been with other men before, but not like this. Not without Steven right by my side, enjoying the show or participating in the fun. I was supposed to leave in ten minutes, and I didn't even know where I was going, who I was seeing, or what the night had in store for me. All I had was a text from him, received an hour before: "Take a shower and be ready to leave by seven. You have a date." Steven had decided to finish up his work at home, but he hadn't given me any more details as I nervously prepared for my mysterious evening out. I had a strong suspicion he'd come home just to watch me squirm. "Just one detail? Please?"

"Sorry, Sam, that's on a need to know basis, and you don't need to know *anything* just yet. What are you doing in the closet, anyway? Your clothes are on the bed." Baffled, I headed to the bedroom to see what he'd laid out for me. *Probably for the best,* I thought, *since I don't even*

129

know where the hell I'm going. To my surprise, what lay before me on the bed was not a nice top and jeans, nor was it a casual dress. Fishnet stockings lay on top of an impossibly short skirt with attached garters and a simple black corset. I laughed a bit, thinking for a moment that surely he must be joking. I know how he enjoys playing tricks on me, and I fall for them every time.

"Come on. What am I *really* wearing?" Steven looked at me sternly, as if he was beginning to lose patience.

"I think I just told you what you're wearing. So how about you quit your yapping and put it on? I'll help you with the corset; you're running late with all this talking." He picked up the corset and stood there, smiling sarcastically, waiting for me to take it from him and put it on. A panic attack nearly overcame me. What in the hell was he doing to me? When we'd met up with other guys before, I'd never really been anxious or freaked out about it. But in all those cases I was, well, *dressed.* In actual clothes, not something that looked like it belonged in a stripper-wear catalog. I gave Steven one last incredulous look, then I slipped the corset on, and he hooked the front and pulled the laces in the back tight. So tight I thought I might pass out.

I stepped carefully into the skirt and gasped as I looked at myself in the mirror and discovered my entire ass was exposed. *Really, Steven?* With an exaggerated sigh, I grabbed the stockings, slipped them on, and requested his assistance in attaching them to the garters. I always did suck at that, particularly while wearing a tight-as-hell corset. He fastened them quickly, slapped my ass, and laughed a rather foreboding laugh. The twinkle in his eye pleased and terrified me all at once.

I stood there in what amounted to little more than lingerie, completely dumbfounded as to how to proceed. It's not like I could leave the house like this. It was still daylight, for God's sake! Where in the hell could I go with this getup on? Steven pointed at my black platform mary janes, and by the time I put them on, he had returned with my wool pea coat. "I know it's hot out," he said with a slight shrug, "but you need to at least wear this until you get there."

"Get *where*, exactly?" I shook my head as I took the coat and put it on with another sigh. He laughed again.

"First of all, stop sighing at me. Second, I'm not telling you where you're going. Head to the bridge, and I'll text you at some point and let you know where to go next."

I stifled another sigh and buttoned up the coat, then I grabbed my purse, stuck my phone inside it, and attempted to remember how to breathe in the hopes of not, well, dying before I got wherever the hell I was going. He grabbed me by the shoulders and looked me in the eyes with a loving smile. "Would I make you do something I knew you'd hate?" His face wrinkled in thought. "Wait. Bad question. Don't answer that. Do you *think* I'm sending you off to be miserable tonight? Because I'm not. You are going to have an amazing time, you just have to trust me. I'll be working for the next few hours, but I'll be thinking of you non-stop."

I nodded my head and smiled weakly. My nerves were overtaking me, but I knew I needed to remain calm so I could drive. I gave him a lingering hug, and he kissed me lightly on the lips, careful not to smudge my makeup. He gave my ass a hard slap as I walked through the door, and he reminded me to check my phone when I got to the bridge.

I got into the car, took my phone out of my purse and put it in my lap, then backed out of the driveway. I took a deep breath and told myself that all would be well. He was clearly quite excited about the night, so something good must be planned. I just needed to trust him and hope for

132

the best. Trusting him was easy, but the hoping for the best part was a bit more of a struggle. Expecting the worst was just my way, and I had to work on changing my thinking. I cranked up the radio and headed out, singing along loudly to "Chains of Love" as I tried to think about anything other than the hours before me.

My phone buzzed just as I got onto the bridge. "Take the Carrollton Exit, North." Nice, Steven. Still no address? Surely he's not making me hang out at one of our usual neighborhood bars in this outfit? I adjusted the rear view mirror to make sure there wasn't a camera crew waiting to jump up and inform me I'd been punk'd. Nope, the backseat was empty. Shit. Onward, to Carrollton.

As I sat nervously at the stop sign to turn onto Carrollton, my phone buzzed again. "Condo across from the party we went to last year." *Oh, crap. What the hell street was that place on?* I drove slowly, pondering where I should turn. As if I remembered the ride home from that party, with its 5 hours of open bar service. Ha! Suddenly I spied a street that looked vaguely familiar, and I quickly turned right. There was the building, but I had no idea how to get inside. It was locked down like Fort Knox from the looks of it – an old warehouse that had been repurposed as high end condos. I drove around the block and parked on the street that ran along the back of the building, then I sat in my car, not sure what the hell to do next.

I saw a family exit the building and walk towards the street, and as they clicked a button on their key fob, an iron gate slowly swung open. Seizing my opportunity to gain access to the building, I grabbed my purse and phone and hopped out of the car, making sure my coat was pulled as far down as it could go as I practically sprinted to the gate. No small feat in my corset and platform heels. I squeezed through just as the gate slid shut, and I slowed down, attempting to walk nonchalantly towards the back door of the building after my awkward run towards the gate. I caught my reflection in the glass doors and had to laugh. It was 95 degrees outside and I was wearing heels, fishnets, and a coat. Jesus, I looked like a call girl. I laughed again, wondering if I'd be receiving an envelope of cash when I arrived at my destination.

The door to the building was unlocked, so I waltzed in like I owned the place, only to quickly realize that I had no fucking clue where I was going. I stood in the lobby pretending to admire a large piece of artwork until I heard my phone buzz a third time. "327." I gulped audibly, looking around with relief that no one was nearby to hear me. Not terribly attractive. I walked slowly to the

134

elevator and pressed the button. A wave of nausea hit me as I realized in about two minutes I'd be finding out what all this was about. As much as I knew he had surely planned something out carefully, not knowing what to expect was getting the best of me. Just as I was beginning to see spots from the surging waves of anxiety crashing over me, the elevator opened. *Pull it together, woman, you've got this.*

I stepped onto the elevator and extended my trembling hand to press the number three. The elevator lurched upward, and so did my dinner. I shook off as much anxiety as I could, and when the elevator opened I walked out into the hallway and followed the sign which indicated that units 316 and up were to the right. I walked all the way to the end of the hallway, laughing to myself that *of course* it would have to be the very farthest condo from the elevator. I reached out, grasped the door knocker, and banged it against the door a little louder than I'd meant to. Damned nerves. After a few torturous moments, the doorknob turned, and the door began to slowly open.

I stood, frozen, as the door finally swung open to reveal a handsome older man. It was hard to estimate his age, but he had a mature demeanor, and he wore a crisp white dress shirt, tie, and slacks. His hair was short and

135

dark, with slight hints of grey throughout. *Where did Steven find this guy?* I thought to myself as I stood there, glued to the floor and smiling awkwardly because I had no idea what else to do. "Come in," he said with a warm smile and an extended arm, as if I didn't know quite how to get into his apartment. I walked past him through the doorway, my knuckles turning white from the death grip I had on my purse. I stood in his living room and nervously looked around.

"You should text Steven and let him know you made it up alright," he suggested. It suddenly occurred to me he hadn't even told me his name. Wow, this is awkward. Do I ask him his name? Do I just wait for it to come up in conversation? Stupid, stupid Sam. I quickly texted Steven to let him know I'd arrived at the condo. I wasn't sure what else to say, as I still hadn't a clue about what was going on. I set my purse down on the bar and stood there wondering what I was supposed to do next. I heard my phone buzz from inside my purse, and I grabbed it, desperate for some clarity. "Do whatever he says. That's an order."

I stood there staring at my phone like a dumbass. *What?* What did that mean? *Whatever he says?* I felt my palms grow sweaty with anxiety and uncertainty. I'd never

136

been in a situation like this without Steven there as my safety net, and I felt completely overwhelmed. Just then, the unnamed man took the phone from my hand, set it down, and guided me down the hall, towards his bedroom. I was a bundle of nerves, and so full of confused thoughts that I didn't know how to act, what to do. All I had was that text. "Do whatever he says." Wow. I took a very deep breath, told myself that Steven knew what he was doing, and what he wanted, and I decided my only option was to just go with it.

The man led me into his bedroom, which was nicely appointed, with rich cherry wood furniture and a lovely four poster king-sized bed. I stood near the doorway, and he motioned for me to come closer. "Take your coat off," he instructed with a gentle, yet authoritative tone. I complied immediately, and he took my coat and laid it on a chair near the bed. He sat on the bed and looked me over for a bit longer than I was comfortable with. I felt quite exposed in the corset, short skirt, and stockings. "Pull your skirt up a bit," he said, and my face immediately flushed to a horrifying shade of beet red. I suddenly realized Steven hadn't given me any panties to wear, and raising my skirt even an inch would leave me totally exposed. "Don't make

137

me ask you again," he said with a somewhat sterner tone, but his eyes still belied a gentle nature.

I thought about the text, and about the fact that Steven had instructed me to obey this stranger. Surely he'd had enough contact with this man to feel comfortable with him. I supposed I should too, so I grasped the bottom of my skirt and pulled it up a bit, until he nodded. "Very good," he said with a smile. I didn't think I'd ever felt quite so exposed, so vulnerable. "Come here," he instructed, and I walked slowly towards him.

He reached out and grabbed my ass firmly, then ran his hands down my legs. It felt so strange, being touched by a man whose name I didn't even know, but I took a deep breath and resolved to just go with it. He wasn't bad looking, and obviously Steven felt he was a trustworthy individual, or I wouldn't be here at all. The man stood up and put his hands behind my head, running them through my hair. "Bend over and put your face on the bed," he said, pushing me down towards the mattress. I did as he instructed, bending at the waist until my face was pressed against the soft sheets.

I jumped when I felt his hand give my ass a hard slap. It was followed by three more slaps in fairly rapid succession, and I attempted to keep breathing and not make a sound. "That's a good girl," he said as he gently rubbed my ass cheek, which surely must have been an angry red by that point. He then slapped the other cheek even harder, again and again until I let out a muffled scream. He laughed a bit then rubbed my welted skin softly. "Steven told me you were tougher than this. We'll have to test that theory, because now I'm not so sure." I found myself audibly gulping for a second time that evening.

I sensed him walking away from me, but I didn't dare move my face from its position on the mattress. He returned, and I felt a hand on my ass, then the sharp sting of what felt like a cane. I let out an embarrassing yelp before attempting to regain my composure. He struck me with it again and again, and I could hear his breathing increase ever so slightly. My breathing sped up too as I attempted to take the pain without screaming. I didn't want to appear fragile, but canes had always been my weakness, and I had a feeling he must have been informed of that fact. He struck my thighs and ass repeatedly and methodically, for so long that I thought I couldn't possibly bear it any more. A part of me wanted so badly to beg him to stop, to let me up, to allow me to run out the door. But I knew I would never do those things; it simply wasn't in my nature to disappoint Steven, *or* to admit defeat.

He struck me again and again, and the pain was like nothing I'd ever experienced. Finally I began to see spots behind my closed eyes, then after a while I felt like I was being slowly wrapped in a cloud as the endorphins kicked in and did their beautiful work on me. I moaned, then whimpered, then sighed, then just *was.* I continued to feel the cane striking me, but it felt like it was cushioned, or I was cushioned, or maybe the world was cushioned. It felt lovely. My breathing grew so slow and steady it probably appeared as though I was asleep. Yet he continued striking me, increasing the speed and intensity with each blow. My entire body trembled with soft waves of pleasure, and I wanted it to never stop.

It took me a few moments to realize the cane had been replaced by hands. He had set the cane down and was gently rubbing my ass and thighs. My nerve endings slowly began to come back to life, and after a while it felt like my skin had been set on fire. His hands were cool and soft and smooth, and the sensation of him caressing me was so comforting that I thought I could fall asleep right there, in this foreign bed with this nameless man next to me. Before I could even consider drifting off, his hands were

140

gone, and without his cool, soothing touch I felt the pain in my welted skin return full force.

I heard the sound of a zipper, felt his hands grasping the front of my hips and yanking me roughly back towards him, then I felt his cock plunging violently into me. I gasped loudly, and he leaned down until his face was next to mine. "You're not going to make a single sound. Not one. Do you understand?" After almost saying yes, I quickly shut my mouth and nodded in affirmation. He resumed his upright position, grabbed my hips roughly with both hands, and began to pound into me, slowly, but with considerable force. I slapped a hand over my mouth instinctively as I almost let out a whimper, and he immediately scolded me. "No cheating. Hands forward, flat on the bed." I slid my hands out in front of me, and with nothing to hold me up, my face was forced back down onto the bed. I bit my lip hard, hoping that wasn't against the rules too.

He continued to fuck me, and neither of us made a sound. Everything in me wanted to scream out; the sensation was too intense to lie there quietly. But I knew I must, so I lay there, breathing as mindfully as I could, and biting my lip until blood trickled down onto the sheets. He quickened his pace, thrusting so hard and fast I thought I'd

141

fly off the other side of the bed. But his hands remained on my hips, pulling me back with each thrust, harder and harder each time. I tasted salt mixed with the coppery flavor of blood, and I realized I had tears streaming down my face and pooling up on the sheets beneath me. I closed my eyes tightly and held my breath, certain I couldn't possibly take much more.

He let out an almost imperceptible grunt, and I felt his cock grow even more rigid for a few moments before he plunged into me one last time and came. He remained inside me for another minute or so, then he released my hips and pulled out. He walked into the bathroom and shut the door, and I stood up, looking with horror at my reflection in the mirror as I pulled my skirt down. I grabbed a tissue off his dresser and blotted away the tears, blood, and mascara. He returned to the bedroom and hardly glanced my way.

"You may go now," he said rather matter-of-factly. I was somewhat taken aback, but then again, the entire night was one unexpected turn after another. "I'll tell Steven you were almost perfect. *Almost.*" With that, he exited the bedroom, and I heard another door open and then shut. Feeling like I was trapped in a strange dream, I wandered up the hallway, grabbed my purse, and hurried out of the apartment. With trembling hands, I texted Steven to let him know I was on my way home. His immediate reply: "Good. You better be ready for me." *Gulp.*

Assignment Two

As tired as I know Steven must have been last night, he sure did give me a superior fucking. I wanted so badly to tell him everything, but he insisted I write it all down so he could read it the next day at work. After I sent him my write-up, I busied myself with chores and errands. I tried not to think about the fact that he'd left this morning with an overnight bag. I hate those fucking overnight bags. They mean he has to leave me for some "very important meeting", and that I have to sleep alone. I know Steven hates them even more, though, so I was determined not to whine about it.

I was standing in Target, agonizing over which flavor of Greek yogurt I should purchase, when my phone vibrated in my pocket. I tossed some blueberry yogurt in the cart and grabbed the phone, hoping it was a text from Steven. To my delight, it was. "I enjoyed reading about your night. You deserve a treat. Remember Ian? Be ready at eight." My face flushed instantly, and I felt a lump forming in my throat. Ian had lived a block or so away from us before he left town for a new job once he'd graduated from college. I'd always had a crush on him, and I'd been pretty vocal to Steven about my admiration for Ian's body. Steven had rolled his eyes more than once as I slowed the car down to enjoy the view as Ian mowed his lawn (shirtless, of course), or when I acted like a silly school girl whenever we had occasion to talk to him. He was far too young for me, but I couldn't help being desperately attracted to him.

I'd even casually mentioned the possibility of a threesome with Ian. Okay, maybe it wasn't so casual. Maybe I actually begged. I might have even emailed Steven a list of all the reasons it was a great idea. I'm not proud, okay? I just had a serious crush, and my *God,* did I want his body. Steven had always responded with something between mild amusement and moderate irritation at my suggestions, so I finally gave up on the idea. Then, alas, Ian moved away. No more lawn-mowing eye candy. No more giggling and averting my eyes when he smiled at me during Neighborhood Watch meetings. It's the only reason I'd ever even gone to those blasted meetings anyway!

I knew Steven and Ian had kept in touch; Steven had been the one who was fairly instrumental in Ian's lucrative career move. I'd chided Steven repeatedly for sending "my man" away, but it *had* been really kind of him to help Ian

145

out. They worked in similar fields, and those connections were vital to Ian, who was just starting out. I wondered why he was back in town, and for how long, and I marveled at this extraordinarily unexpected turn of events. I felt like a kid at Christmas, and I was *very* ready to unwrap my present. I glanced at my watch and let a few expletives slip from my mouth when I discovered eight o'clock was unacceptably far away.

I rushed through the rest of my shopping, then I headed home to put away the groceries and take a bath. I sank into the hot, bubbly water and closed my eyes, imagining (not for the first time) being in bed with Ian, kissing him, running my hands across his chest, slipping his pants off to reveal what was almost certainly a remarkable cock. A cock that absolutely *must* fuck me. Preferably a few times. Dear Lord, I'd fantasized about that boy for years. I couldn't believe those fantasies were going to come true. I knew Steven was hard at work, two states away, and I smiled as I pondered how sweet he'd been to set this up for me. I smiled again as I thought about all the filthy ways I'd thank him upon his return.

After my bath, I finished up some laundry (ah, the excitement!) and then settled into my favorite chair to read for a while. Nothing like a bit of corny vampire fiction to

146

pass the time, right? It was finally nearing eight o'clock, and I hadn't heard a word from Steven. I put on a little bit of makeup, and I decided to wear a simple black knit dress and some wedge sandals. I didn't have a clue where I'd be going, but I figured that would work pretty much anywhere. Just as I began to panic about what time I should leave, I received a text from Steven. "Ian will pick you up in ten minutes." My nerves went into instant overdrive, and I literally became dizzy with anticipation. I checked my makeup one more time, grabbed my purse, and decided to wait in the living room.

After what seemed more like ten hours than ten minutes, a car pulled up, and the doorbell rang. *Deep breaths*, I told myself. Passing out would not be a great way to start the date, nor would panting like I'd just run a marathon. I calmed myself down a bit just in time to open the door and behold the amazing spectacle that was Ian. *Damn.* Had he gotten even hotter? I owed Steven for this. Big time. Ian gave me a hug and a huge smile, and we got into his car and began to catch up as he drove. He'd been enjoying his work tremendously, but he missed home, and he said more than a few times that he was really happy to see me. Trust me, the feeling was mutual. I felt slightly guilty for silently wishing we could skip the formalities of

147

drinks and just fast forward to the part where I fucked him senseless. Then again, drinks *did* sound nice...

We parked close to a small dive bar downtown. Ian explained that he was in town for work, and that he was actually staying at a hotel right around the corner from the bar. I detected a little wicked smile as he casually mentioned this fact, and I hoped that meant he'd be ready to stroll on over to the hotel after a bit of drinking and chatting. I didn't think I could keep my hands off him much longer, and I certainly didn't want him to keep his hands off *me*.

Ian held open the large wooden door to the bar, and I walked in as he followed behind me. It was dimly lit, smoky, and not terribly crowded. A jukebox in the corner was playing Devo, which seemed a rather odd choice, given the clientele. We sat at the bar, and I ordered a vodka tonic. Ian ordered some import beer I'd never heard of, and to my surprise, the bar actually had it. We sipped our drinks and caught up a bit more; I told him about the recent goings-on in the neighborhood since he'd moved, and I admitted I hadn't been to a single Neighborhood Watch meeting since he'd left town. He told me about his job, his new apartment, and a girl he'd been seeing until very recently.

I couldn't help gawking just a bit as I sat there with Ian. He wasn't even my *type,* but I had always been drawn to him; he was slightly tan, muscular, and had tousled dirty blond hair. His eyes were icy blue and almost didn't even seem real. He wore a snug-fitting t shirt and dark, baggy jeans, and I couldn't help thinking about how badly I wanted to divest him of those cumbersome articles of clothing. He smelled amazing, almost intoxicating, and I found myself utterly unable to stay focused on our conversation.

After what seemed like hours of chit chat, drinking, and flirting, Ian leaned towards me. I thought he was going to kiss me, but instead he whispered into my ear. "Want to head to my hotel?" His breath on my ear tickled and gave me a sudden chill. I rubbed my arms, willing the goose bumps to disappear, and I nodded and smiled at him. I tried to appear nonchalant, but I was *so* ready to kiss him, to touch him, to feel him inside me. Ian paid our tab, and we were on our way. I was a bundle of nerves as we walked around the corner to his hotel. As we rode the elevator, he smiled almost shyly at me. "You look amazing, by the way," he said before looking down at the floor. I eyed the emergency button on the wall of the elevator, and I briefly considered pushing it and having my way with him right then and there.

We made our way to Ian's hotel room, and he excused himself to get some ice. He told me to make myself comfortable, so I slipped my shoes off and sat in the chair next to the bed. It occurred to me I hadn't checked my phone at all, so I grabbed it, wondering if Steven had texted me. It just so happened that he *had.* "Oh, by the way, there's to be no touching. At all. But I want you both to come. Don't disappoint me." I nearly dropped the phone upon the revelation of this new development. *Evil fucking mastermind of soul-crushing torturous nonsense!* My God, Steven was being particularly sadistic. Last night, with its humiliating and quite painful twist, and now this? Dangling this hot piece of ass in front of me, and I can't even touch? I'd have smiled at the demented beauty of it, had I not been so utterly, completely frustrated.

The door opened, and in came Ian with a bucket of ice and a broad smile. "Did Steven text you?" he asked with a strange expression on his face.

"He did. God, Ian, I'm sorry, but…"

"No, Sam," he quickly interjected. "I knew the rules. It's not a problem. Let's make the best of it, okay?"

I sat there, even more stunned than before. So Steven had told him up front he could take me to his hotel room, but neither of us could touch each other? And he *agreed* to this? Were all the men in my life either insane or evil? Surely they were out to drive *me* out of my mind. I sighed heavily, set my phone down on the nightstand, and resigned myself to enjoying the night as much as possible, despite the fact that I couldn't do a single thing I'd fantasized about all day.

A wave of awkwardness hit me as I realized the extent to which this night was *not* going as I'd hoped and planned. It was almost as though I'd never been with a man before; I had no idea what to do. Fortunately, Ian seemed a bit better prepared. At least *he'd* gotten the memo earlier and had known what to expect. He smiled at me, then motioned for me to sit next to him on the bed. I rose from the chair and sat next to him, careful not to sit so close to him that we touched. *Damn*, this was going to be difficult. I breathed in his scent once again, and every part of me wanted to jump on top of him, tear his clothes off, and do unthinkable things to him. Instead, I just sat there, looking at him and smiling nervously.

Ian finally ended the awkward silence. "I've wanted you since the day we met, Sam," he said, looking at me with an intensity that took my breath away. "I certainly never expected to be alone in a hotel room with you, that's for sure." He smiled, and it was obvious he was exerting a good bit of self-control to not reach out and touch me.

"I guess we should make the best of it, then," I replied, shaking my head and trying not to laugh at the absurdity of the situation. I stood up and pulled my dress over my head, then tossed it onto the chair beside the bed. Ian took that as his cue to do the same, and he removed his shirt, then his jeans. I was certain there must be drool on my chin as I observed him disrobe. He was a god; chiseled to perfection and stunningly beautiful in all his unclothed glory. Steven truly *was* an evil genius. This was torture. I climbed back onto the bed, resting against the headboard as Ian looked me over admiringly. His hand found its way to his cock, and he began to stroke it slowly and gently. I thought I might die.

"I want to see you touch yourself," Ian said, staring at my body as he rubbed his cock. I slid my panties off and ran my hands up my legs, spreading my pussy open for him. His hand began to work his cock faster, and I slipped a finger inside myself, using my other hand to rub my clit. I was so turned on I thought I'd explode, but I continued to put on a show for him as I enjoyed the one he was

152

performing for me. My eyes devoured every inch of his body, and every time he moaned my desire for him grew. I watched him intently as he masturbated for me, and I imagined him plunging his cock into me, making me scream, making me come. I wondered if he was imagining the same thing.

We sat there on the bed, dangerously close, touching ourselves as we watched each other intently. I thought I'd feel silly, or awkward, but the scene before me was so hot that none of that even mattered. Ian began to moan loudly, and his grip on his cock tightened as he stroked himself faster. My pace quickened along with his, and waves of pleasure washed over me, bringing me closer and closer to orgasm. Ian's entire body shuddered violently, and with one more stroke he exploded. All over my stomach. This sudden, unexpected bit of intimacy threw me over the edge, and I cried out as my climax overtook me. We sat there for a few minutes, just looking at each other and catching our breath. Ian finally got up and grabbed a towel for me, playfully tossing it in my direction. I wiped myself off, smiling as I looked down at the mess he'd made on me. I realized it was probably as close as I'd ever get to fucking him.

We dressed, and he drove me home; neither of us was quite sure what to say, so we listened to the radio and didn't even attempt any small talk. My phone buzzed, and of course, it was Steven. "Hug him goodbye. Wouldn't want to be rude!" Just as I read it, Ian pulled up in front of my house. He walked me to the door, and without meaning to seem so enthusiastic, I threw my arms around him and hugged him tightly. His body felt so warm, so inviting, so good, that all I wanted to do was drag him into the house and make him hold me all night. Alas, it wasn't in the cards (or the texts), so I finally released my grip on him and thanked him for an interesting evening.

"I, uh, hope I can see you again sometime if I make it back this way," he said with an understandably puzzled look on his face. It had been a confusing night, to say the least, and I was glad he'd been willing to go along with Steven's unusual request. I nodded in agreement, and then I went into the house and shut the door. I peeked through the window to watch him walk to his car and drive away. I was exhausted, and still a little tipsy, so I got ready for bed, making sure to text Steven before falling asleep.

"You're the devil. I love you."

Assignment Three

Steven and I had an amazing few days together after he returned home from his brief business trip. I gave him a hundred kinds of hell about the terrible, no-good, mean trick he'd played on me; for giving him a hard time about it, he beat my ass until it was a hundred shades of red. The weekend was suddenly upon us, and Steven actually had those two days off, so we made the very most of every moment. He mentioned Ian several times, asking each time for me to tell him all the things I'd have done, had I been allowed. It made for some tantalizingly hot moments between us as I described in agonizing detail all the things I'd wanted to do to Ian, and to have Ian do to me.

Alas, the weekend ended, and Steven had another late night at work. I was riding high on the phenomenal several days we'd had, and the last thing I expected was another assignment. When my phone buzzed, I assumed Steven was simply asking me to get dinner ready, or telling me he loved me. Instead, I received another set of instructions. "Working really late. Feel just *terrible* about the Ian thing.

Want to make it up to you. How's a threesome sound? No holds barred. Room 1217, The W. Now."

A smile spread across my face as I read Steven's text. We'd had quite a few threesomes before, but I'd never had one on my own, and I was instantly intrigued. The thought of being taken by two guys, then telling Steven all about it, almost made up for not being able to touch Ian. *Almost.* I took the quickest shower possible, threw on a comfy, yet sexy dress, and hauled ass downtown. Parking was a bitch, but I finally made it to the hotel. I was full of anticipation as I entered the elevator. I blinked stupidly as I stared at the panel of buttons, looking for the one I needed to press. There was no twelfth floor. *Crap.* I texted Steven. "Did you send me the wrong room number? There's no 12th floor!!!" I exited the elevator and sat in the lobby, awaiting his reply.

"Silly Sam. You must be at the wrong W. Only *one* has twelve floors. Better hustle. They're waiting on you."

I stared at my phone, completely flabbergasted. I inquired at the front desk about the other hotel, and the clerk gave me the address. She mentioned there was a shuttle from one location to the other, so that guests could use the amenities at each. Not mentioning the fact that I

156

wasn't *quite* a guest, I had her point the way to the shuttle, and in ten minutes I was standing in front of the correct hotel.

I checked the time and hurried to the elevator, letting out a relieved sigh as I pressed the number twelve and felt the elevator lurch upwards. I adjusted my dress, attempted to check out my makeup in the reflection of the metal panel, and took a deep breath, ready to have some fun with the two guys who were apparently anxiously awaiting my arrival. I felt like a bit of a whore, and I kind of liked it.

The elevator grumbled to a stop at the twelfth floor, and I hopped out and followed the signs leading me to the correct room number. Once there, I knocked gently on the door and awkwardly called out, "It's Sam – you guys in there?" God, I can be such a dork sometimes. I was nervous, though, and when I'm nervous I sometimes get a bit awkward. I figured they'd gladly overlook it.

The door opened, and two older women in black lingerie greeted me. Without even realizing it, I took half a step back and peered up and down the hall, as if perhaps I had knocked on the wrong door, and perhaps these ladies were awaiting someone else. The brunette grabbed hold of my wrist and pulled me into the room with a smile. My heart, among other parts, sank as I realized Steven had played yet another trick on me.

I reached into my phone to shoot off a quick text as the ladies stood far too close to me, looking me over carefully. "Dirty pool, Sir," I typed quickly and hit send, and an immediate reply came back. "Get to it, then." Followed by a smiley face. *That bastard.* Steven knew my interest in women was purely non-sexual, and despite the fact that I'd indulged him in a few threesomes with me and another girl, it just personally did nothing for me. My only enjoyment was in pleasing him, in seeing him have a good time. I knew he expected me to follow through with this, though, so I swallowed my pride, tossed my purse onto a nearby chair, and put an arm around each of the ladies.

JoAnne and Sandy were their names, and they were quite happy to prattle on about their lives as they made me a cocktail from the mini bar under the large flat panel television in the hotel room's enormous armoire. They were a couple here on vacation for their tenth anniversary. Both had been married to men, and had been best friends until they found their husbands were cheating on them with a coworker and a neighbor. JoAnne and Sandy found solace in each other, and then found quite a bit more than that, as soon they were a couple. Ten years later, they found themselves seeking out a little added spice via an online personals ad. And well, thanks to Steven, apparently I was that spice.

I stifled a laugh at the sick absurdity of the situation, at the crafty way in which Steven had completely fooled me into thinking he was serving me up to two hot men. I realized I'd probably tricked myself, just because that's what I'd *hoped* it would be. But he knew that too, and he was loving every minute of this "big reveal." I figured it was probably making his late night at work more palatable, and despite the circumstances, I was happy to oblige.

I set my glass down and climbed onto the duvet between the two lace-clad ladies, who both seemed more than eager to welcome me into their bed. JoAnne ran her hand through my hair, then pushed it aside to reveal my bare neck, which she kissed softly at first, then harder, with more urgency. Sandy wasted no time in pulling the thin straps of my dress down my shoulders, exposing my breasts. The two women explored my breasts, arms, and belly in a leisurely fashion, as if they had absolutely nothing to do but revel in that one moment. I smiled to myself as I lay back on the bed and pondered how very different this experience was without two erect cocks waiting impatiently to plunge into whatever orifice they

159

could make their way to first. Perhaps this wasn't such a bad task after all.

Their kisses and caresses slowly travelled the length of my body, from my face and throat down to my toes, and soon my dress was in a crumpled ball on the floor. The women stopped every few moments to kiss each other passionately before returning their collective attention to me. After three or four journeys up and down the length of my body, they settled on either side of me, their faces near my hips, and they smiled wickedly into each others' eyes, then peeled my panties off and tossed them onto the floor, near my crumpled dress. I looked down at them, but before long my head fell back onto the mattress and my eyes were rolling back into my skull as wave after wave of ridiculous pleasure struck me. I'd heard time and time again how a woman knows another woman's body better than a man does, but that claim had never rung true, based on the few experiences I'd had. These women, however, knew what they were doing. And with both of them focusing their complete attention on me, I thought I might pass out from orgasm overdose.

I screamed out, so loudly it shocked me, as I felt a mouth encircle my clit again and again, and a hand expertly working its way inside me, finding just the right spot with each thrust. Two more hands caressed my pubic bones, my hips, my ass, as I writhed around on the bed like a madwoman. When I'd entered the room, I was certain I'd be expected to please both these women; it hadn't occurred to me that they both wanted a fresh body to explore, to tease, to bring to orgasm. And that they did, like nothing I'd felt before, and I was in awe. All they wanted was to please me; it was quite the reversal of my people-pleasing nature, to just lie back and accept this gift. But that I did, until I was positive I'd die if I came one more time. I hesitantly reached down with both hands and grasped at their heads, pushing them away from my sweaty, trembling body.

JoAnne and Sandy understood immediately, and they slid up towards the head of the bed, lying on either side of me and gently stroking my cheeks and my hair as I lay there panting and shivering in the aftermath of that unexpected encounter. Their arms surrounded me and they held me close as they leaned across me and ever-so-softly kissed. Their eyes beamed with love for each other, and in that moment I was humbled to be part of their anniversary celebration. I wasn't sure what Steven had expected when he offered me up to these two women, but I was sincerely glad he'd decided to do it.

After a few more minutes of basking in the afterglow, I felt it was time to make myself scarce so the ladies could have some private time. Part of me wanted to stay and watch the show, but a bigger part of me knew Steven would be getting home soon, and I was anxious to see him, and to pick up things with him where I'd left off with my two new friends. I kissed them each on the cheek and wished them a happy anniversary, then I stepped quickly into my dress, slipped my panties on, and grabbed my purse. They were already lost in each other by the time I made it to the door and walked out into the hallway.

On the elevator ride back to the lobby, I texted Steven. "Mission accomplished. On my way home." By the time I'd reached the lobby he had replied. "OMW too. Can't wait to ravish you. Or are you spent?" I smiled and slipped my phone back into my purse; he could wait a while for my answer. The shuttle ride back to the other hotel seemed to take ages, and I couldn't wait to get home. Finally, the bus pulled into the hotel's drop-off area, and I practically leapt out onto the concrete and sprinted to my car. When I arrived home, I saw Steven's car in the driveway and bounded into the house to tell him of my evening's adventures, and to find out what he had in store for me. After his long day at work, I was certain he had

some major steam to blow off. And that, he surely did.
Three times.

Assignment Four

Steven was working in town for several days, and I couldn't have been happier. He arrived home in a particularly good mood after a meeting with the board of directors of something or other, and he said he wanted to celebrate the completion of the project he'd been working on. I suddenly understood the reason for the spring in his step, and I threw my arms around him and kissed him. My lips had barely grazed his when I felt something being placed in my hand. A shopping bag.

"Go put this on. We're going for dinner and drinks, my love!" He gave me a swat on the ass as I broke from his embrace and sauntered sassily towards the bedroom. I knew Steven enjoyed dressing me up to go out, and I just knew it would be something sexy, and as much as I sometimes hated to admit it, I *did* enjoy wearing sexy clothes for him. I reached into the bag to fine a sheer black sheath dress, cut rather short, with a black lace bra and matching lace panties. With a huge grin spreading across my face, I donned them and put on some makeup. I normally didn't wear red lipstick, but it seemed quite fitting, given the elegant, yet sexy dress. I slipped on some red stilettos to complete the look.

"Gorgeous!" Steven practically yelled out when I returned to the living room. He was still in the suit he'd worn all day, and while his 5 o'clock shadow looked more like a midnight shadow, and his suit was a bit rumpled from the day's work, he looked sexy as hell. I hopped into his lap and gave him a lingering hug, then we were off to dinner. I wondered where we'd end up, and to my surprise we ended up downtown, at a posh new nightspot that served appetizers and designer cocktails. It wasn't our kind of place, as we normally preferred a few beers at a neighborhood bar, but we were in celebratory mode, so the setting seemed appropriate.

We sat at a small table near the bar, and Steven ordered a cheese plate, some chargrilled oysters, and two dirty martinis. I was almost afraid to eat; I knew my dress must have been pricey since Steven had carefully removed the tags before handing the bag over to me. Once the food arrived, though, I scarfed down oysters, cheese, and crackers like I was wearing jeans and a t shirt. They were delicious. We sipped our martinis, and Steven filled me in on his meeting, and on the fact that he had a week of vacation coming to him after a job well done. We mused

165

over the possibilities, and we settled on some time relaxing at the beach. I didn't care where we went, as long as we were together. We were more than ready to spend a week enjoying each other, without cell phones and constant emails and last-minute work travels interfering.

As we sat and talked about our vacation, it suddenly occurred to me that my little assignments may also be coming to an end with the conclusion of Steven's project. While we always found ways to have fun and keep life interesting, I felt a bit melancholy at the thought of no more texts sending me to undisclosed locations to do goodness-knows-what. Steven must have detected the hint of sadness in my eye, because he leaned over to me and whispered into my ear. "There's a note in your purse. Go freshen up in the ladies' room and read it. I'll order us another round." I perked up immediately and almost jumped up from the table to search out the restroom. Steven never did disappoint.

I entered the restroom, locked myself in one of the luxuriously large stalls, and tore the note from my purse. "My friend at the warehouse condo told me you're a bit on the shy side. We need to work on that. Take off your bra and panties and meet me at the bar." I felt my face flush once again. Sure, we didn't really know anyone who

166

frequented this bar, and sure, it was pretty dimly lit out there. But the dress was *so* sheer. I was sure to shock, offend, and potentially horrify someone, and I wasn't too thrilled with that notion.

I realized I couldn't have it both ways; just moments before, I was wistfully regretting that these tasks might be coming to an end. Now here I was, hiding in the restroom stall and wishing there was a window through which I could shimmy and run to the car. I knew it would please him tremendously for me to follow through, and I knew that would in turn please *me*. I shook my head and half-smiled at the irony of my life, then I slipped off my bra and panties and tucked them into my purse.

I exited the restroom and began walking towards Steven, who had relocated to the bar and seemed to be eagerly awaiting my emergence from the ladies room. I noticed him shaking his head in disapproval, and I realized I was instinctively covering my breasts with my purse. I lowered my purse to my hip, thanked the gods of interior design that trendy bars had low lighting, and walked as confidently as possible to Steven. I set my purse on the bar and embraced him, and after a soft, sweet kiss, he gently pushed me away. "You're cheating again – you can't tuck yourself against my chest all night. Have a seat." I sighed, nodded, and took the seat next to him, where a martini was awaiting me.

Steven and I chatted about vacation options, and as he pulled up resort details on his phone, I found myself expectantly watching the door, not sure what might happen next. Steven slipped his arm around my waist and pulled me closer to him. "Just you and me tonight, Sam. I hope that's okay with you." I nodded eagerly with a smile, and he smirked back at me evilly. "That doesn't mean I can't have a little fun with your…situation…should the opportunity arise. In fact, those men in the corner seem to be checking you out. Why don't you give them a little more to appreciate." He spun my barstool around until I was directly facing the small group of men standing about fifteen feet away. I could tell from their expressions they suddenly realized the extent to which the dress revealed my breasts. My face warmed again as I saw them nodding in my direction and whispering to each other.

I looked down and focused all of my attention on my martini, and it was gone within seconds. Steven laughed and ordered me another. "This is your last drink, Sam. Can't rely on martinis to get over your shyness." He held the barstool in place so that I continued to face the men as they stared at me and Steven prattled off the details of our various resort options. I heard wonderful words like massage, candlelit dinner, moonlight stroll, but all I could focus on was the three pairs of eyes staring at me from across the room. Then Steven's mouth was whispering into my ear, "Uncross your legs – they want a show? Give them a show." I thought I'd die. Steven's hand gently tugged at my leg as he kissed my neck, and my knees were suddenly just far enough apart for it to be obvious I was wearing no panties. I felt Steven's hand gently caress my breast as he kissed my neck once again, and I was certain we'd be kicked out of the bar any minute. Save for the three very observant men, no one else seemed any the wiser that an impromptu peep show was taking place.

I looked up at the men, who were no longer engaged in conversation; they were standing there, drinks in hand, just staring at us. I forced myself to fix my gaze on them as I felt Steven's hand trail down from my breast to the hem of my dress. His hand slipped up my thigh, taking my dress with it, and I gasped as I felt his fingers slip inside me. He kept them there for just a moment, then slid his hand back to my knee, pushing my legs closed. I was shocked, and actually a little bit aroused by how such a small gesture seemed to leave the three observers in complete awe. I suppose they weren't used to that sort of audacity; and honestly, neither was I. I felt a little rush of adrenaline from the unexpected show we'd put on, and I suppose Steven did as well. He tossed a few bills on the bar, grabbed my hand, and led me quickly out the front door. I was almost certain I saw him turn and smile at our admirers on the way out.

I began to walk to the car, but he yanked me in the direction of the side of the building. It must have been the spot smokers congregated, as the stale smell of cigarettes hung in the air, but no one was present at the moment. Steven wasted no time in unzipping his suit pants, hiking my dress up, and ramming his cock deep into my exposed pussy. The pressure of him forced me into the rough brick wall and I gasped, more out of concern for my dress than out of pain. After a few moments, though, I forgot all about my dress. Steven's hands found my clit, and he always knew just how to touch me. Without even realizing it, I screamed out, not even caring if anyone heard, or if anyone happened upon us. My mind was lost in him, and in moonlit walks on the beach, and in fucking in the waves while the other beachgoers slept.

Assignment Five

"One last assignment for you, Sam," Steven said, practically springing into the room with an empty suitcase and tossing it onto the floor at the foot of the bed. "I just finished my last bit of paperwork, and it's time to head out. Get to packing!"

"Now?" I replied, shocked. I'd thought we needed to at least wait until the weekend, but apparently the weekend was coming a day early. I was thrilled, but suddenly panic-stricken at the thought of not having a day or two to prepare and make my packing list.

"Now. It's time to be spontaneous. Throw some stuff in the bag, we won't need much. We'll grab food once we get settled in – we just need some clothes, swimsuits, maybe a riding crop and some handcuffs..." Steven's voice trailed off as he pondered the possibilities, and I smiled. We'd be 10 minutes tops from the nearest Target; if I forgot something, we'd *probably* live. I packed as quickly as possible, then took a quick shower and was ready to go. After a warm hug and a passionate kiss promising many exhilarating things to come, we were in the car and on the way to the beach.

During our four hour drive through a long and boring stretch of tree-lined interstate, we sang along to the radio and I smiled as I fantasized about a glorious week to enjoy Steven without the constant work interruptions that had plagued us. He'd promised to check his email and voice mail only once a day, and he assured me this was not a problem, that someone was handling all urgent matters for him back at the office. He teased me with all the details of the resort, which sounded more luxurious than any place we'd ever stayed, and as we got closer I thought I'd burst with excitement. While the heated pool sounded amazing for nighttime swims, and while I really *could* go for a massage on the beach under a palapa, what I really wanted was uninterrupted time with Steven. All the rest was lagniappe – much appreciated, but lagniappe nonetheless.

We finally arrived at our destination, and after checking in to the hotel we had dinner at the Asian fusion restaurant on site. Steven fed me eel rolls and spicy crawfish rolls as he complimented me on how well I'd handled all the tasks he'd given me over the past few weeks. He smiled as he told me it had made his long hours of work go by more quickly, devising wicked plans, then imagining me acting out his every whim. He admitted he thought I'd bail that very first night; he knew how far

172

outside my comfort zone it was to let a stranger have his way with me, and he was proud of me for going through with it. He also took the opportunity to tease me once again about Ian. "The one who got away," I said, exaggeratedly shaking my head wistfully and staring off into to the distance. Steven laughed at me and slapped my arm playfully.

"Ready for the beach?" Steven asked once our plates were cleared of all traces of sushi. I felt more like a beached *whale* after all that rice, but the weather was balmy and absolutely perfect for a sunset stroll along the edge of the water. Perhaps it would also be perfect for some other outdoor activities a bit later. We stopped at our room to change into our swimsuits, and to kiss, and to kiss some more, and then I forgot about the beach altogether. As I began to unlace Steven's board shorts, he grabbed my hand and stopped me. "As much as I would love to rip your clothes off right this minute, we *really* don't want to miss that gorgeous sunset." While I cared very little about the sunset, no matter how gorgeous it may be, I relented and followed Steven out onto the terrace. First floor suites at this resort must be tremendously expensive, I thought as I admired the cushioned lounge furniture on our own private patio which led right to the beach. We deserved this vacation, though, so I wasn't going to worry about money. Not this time. Steven took my hand in his and led me to the wooden bridge which deposited us a few feet from the water's edge. The tide was coming in, the sun was setting, and I couldn't wait to dip my toes in the warm surf.

I pulled my shoes off and tossed them at the foot of the bridge. Steven scooped me up and ran into the water, and for a second I thought he might throw me into an oncoming wave. I screamed and held him tightly; while the water looked inviting, I wasn't quite in the mood for a swim. Still holding me, he kissed me deeply, and I felt loved like never before. The past few hours had been bliss, and I couldn't wait to spend the whole week together, enjoying each other with no stress or obligations weighing us down.

I felt Steven's phone vibrating in his pocket, and he lowered me to the ground to check it. I frowned at him, pretty sure it wasn't his allotted hour to check on work. Since it wasn't even the weekend yet, I decided to cut him some slack. He sent off a quick text in reply, and he smiled widely at me. "No worries," he said, "I'll put my phone away right now. Let's head back to the room for a minute so I can get rid of this thing." With that, we walked back to the patio and into the suite. Steven slid the glass door shut, smiled at me, and told me he'd only be a minute. I figured

174

that was code for needing time to call the office, so I swung the bedroom door open to hop into bed and wait for him. My breathing nearly stopped as I looked into the bedroom to find Ian half reclining on the pillows with a huge grin on his face.

I stammered and sputtered for an embarrassingly long period of time, then finally uttered quite awkwardly, "Uhhhh, what are *you* doing here, Ian?" Ian laughed, knowing I must have been completely taken aback by his presence in my bed.

"Steven found out I was here for business til tonight. I think he pulled some pretty big strings to get you guys out here a day early. He really loves you, Sam."

"Don't I know it," I replied. I stood there in the doorway, still smiling awkwardly, not sure what to do. After what seemed like hours, Steven came up behind me and slid his arms around my waist.

"What are you doing just standing here, silly girl? Wouldn't you rather be doing something else? By the way, I hope you don't mind if I join you." He smiled at me, almost shyly.

"I wouldn't have it any other way," I replied, then kissed him deeply, forgetting for a moment about our guest.

After a few minutes, Steven released his grasp on me and guided me towards the bed, following closely behind. I crawled tentatively into bed next to Ian, and he sat up and slipped his hand behind my neck, pulling me toward him. In no time his mouth was pressed firmly against mine, and the electricity between us was palpable. All the pent up sexual tension from our previous encounter came flooding back, and I found myself instinctively pulling his shirt over his head, kissing his neck and chest, running my hands all over his muscular form.

I stopped suddenly and turned back toward Steven, not wanting him to feel left out. He shook his head, smiling, and pushed me back towards Ian. Again my body took hold of me and I was not shy, not afraid, I was nothing but wanting, craving, desiring. I unzipped his jeans, pulling them down and tossing them onto the floor, and his boxer briefs quickly followed. My mouth explored his stomach, his thighs, and finally his fully erect cock. He moaned and raised his hips from the bed; he'd clearly been wanting this as much as I had. I licked and sucked him as he panted and grasped the side of the bed. Then he shuddered a bit, flipped me onto my back, yanked my swimsuit off in one quick motion, and pressed himself against me.

I began to see stars as Ian's body slid over mine, rubbing against me from head to toe. I realized I'd been holding my breath since I landed on my back, and I nearly laughed. I was still in shock, in awe, of what was transpiring, and I literally had to remind myself to breathe. I felt his breath against my clit and thought that alone might make me come. Steven appeared in front of me, smiling and undressed and clearly ready for some attention. I hungrily reached out for him, pulled his hips towards me and took his cock into my eager mouth. The combination of newness and familiarity was intoxicating, and I wanted them both, and I wanted more and more and more of it all. I was giddy with love, and with lust, and with desire for both men, and I again had to remind myself…breathe…

Ian's mouth on my clit, his fingers gently delving into my pussy, were too much for me to bear, and I cried out with Steven's cock still plunging into my throat. I climaxed again and again, and I didn't want it to stop, but I also didn't know how much more I could take of this overwhelming ecstasy. Finally Ian came up for air and kissed me hard; his intentions were evident in the way he pressed his lips against mine, the way his tongue explored my mouth urgently. He moved closer to me, and I felt his cock dip into me, ever-so-tentatively at first, and then faster

177

and harder until I was breathless and moaning without fear of anyone on the other side of the wall hearing us.

Steven motioned to Ian, and it was apparent they'd discussed the logistics of our encounter. Ian immediately grasped my hips and flipped me over on top of him, then guided my body back and forth onto his cock. He threw his head back and closed his eyes for a moment, then looked at me and smiled. I felt Steven position himself behind me, and I gasped in anticipation of what I knew was coming. Steven's cock pressed itself into my ass and I cried out as he plunged into me just as I pulled away from Ian. We kept up this rhythm, all three of us moaning almost in sync as I fucked Ian and Steven fucked me, and it felt like perfect harmony, perfect bliss. Steven then held my hips down so that I couldn't retreat; I was on top of Ian, with his cock as deep in my pussy as it could get, and as Steven held me there he began to fuck my ass more forcefully. It was pleasure and pain and an intensity I'd never felt before, and I felt like I was splitting in two. But I loved it. Ian began to moan in a way I hadn't heard yet, and I realized the extent of pleasure he was experiencing as I knelt on top of him while being fucked by Steven. Steven's moans grew deeper too, and I realized I was screaming right along with them. Just as I began to see stars and feel my entire body shudder and begin to melt, both men exploded inside me. I collapsed onto Ian, and Steven collapsed onto me, and we didn't move for who-knows-how-long.

Finally I slid over onto the bed next to Ian, and Steven in turn lay next to me. They both caressed my face and hair as we drifted off to sleep. I didn't wake up until the sun had come up. I was quite surprised, as I'd expected Ian would be long gone by then, but he was curled up behind me, holding me as I held onto Steven. The sound of the waves was so soothing, I felt like I could lie there all day, but the suite phone rang, rousing me from my thoughts. Apparently Steven had scheduled that massage a little *too* early. Not quite sure how to handle saying my goodbyes to Ian, I snuck out of bed, dressed, and headed to the spa.

Two hours of total relaxation and pampering later, I returned to our suite, wondering if Steven might be sneaking in some work while I was away. To my surprise, I found him and Ian, seated at the dining room table having a few beers and engaged in a lively conversation. Noticing my raised eyebrows, Steven jumped up and greeted me with a hug and a deep kiss. "I hope you don't mind, Sam. I woke up late last night and came up with several new tasks for you, and I think we might need Ian to stay a few days to help out with them. You didn't mind that, did you?"

"No. Not at all," I replied, smiling slyly at them both and grabbing a beer from the fridge. Yes, this would be the best vacation ever.

Extreme Submission:

Stories of Sex on the Edge

By

Audra Morgan

Extreme Submission: Stories of Sex on the Edge

Copyright © 2012 by Audra Morgan

Audra can be contacted by email at

AudraMorganBooks@gmail.com

Kidnapped

I stepped out onto the wet street, looking both ways with a sense of uneasy anticipation. It had rained as I browsed the gallery, with its intriguing combination of surrealist artwork and rusted metal sculptures. I had stared at the painting near the rear stairwell until my eyes began to tear up. The image of gnarled demons pulling two screaming men down into the pits of hell lingered in my mind. I found it strangely terrifying, but the colors were so vivid that I couldn't look away.

Although I'd spent over twenty years wandering about the French Quarter, Royal Street seemed almost foreign to me as I slowly stepped from one rain puddle to the next. The sky was deep grey, and thunder echoed softly in the distance. I smiled to myself as a memory arose of being on this same street at fifteen, running through a rainstorm to shop for tarot cards and patchouli incense. The memory seemed foreign to me now too. It was another me, as if I was remembering a movie I'd seen, not something I'd actually experienced. Shaking off those unnerving thoughts, I zipped up my jacket and glanced across the street in search of another interesting shop to peruse.

183

Before I could take another step, everything went dark. I realized a hood had been pulled over my head, and I felt hands on my shoulders, then on my collarbone, dragging me backwards, shoving me to the left, then tossing me into a vehicle. "Don't move, and don't make a sound." The voice was muffled by the thick cloth pulled tightly over my ears. The car reeked of smoke, and I coughed and tugged at the hood. "I said don't make a sound, Bitch!" Suddenly I was face down on the seat, my hands yanked behind me and my wrists tied together roughly. "Not another sound!" My heart was pounding so hard that I thought I might tumble off the seat and onto the floor. The car bouncing as it sped down the bumpy streets didn't help matters. I tried to breathe, tried to stay calm, and tried like hell not to cough.

After what felt like hours, the car lurched to a stop, and the front door opened and slammed shut again. I heard two male voices, then the back door opened, and I was yanked out by the rope binding my wrists. Two large hands pushed me forward and I stumbled along, trying to keep myself upright. I had no idea where I was or where I was being lead. My mind went momentarily blank as I felt the rain begin to come down again, soaking my hair through the hood and running down my arms and off my fingertips. I attempted to focus on those raindrops instead of on the abject terror creeping up my spine. I tripped over a threshold and realized we had entered a building; it was warm and had a stale aroma, like no one had used it in quite some time. Although I regained my balance and continued walking, the hands kept pushing me forward, as if daring me to fall. I was suddenly yanked back by my shoulder and shoved to the left, and my shoulder banged into what must have been a door frame as we entered another room. The hands pushed me one more time then released me long enough to slam the door shut.

I heard whispers, then I was grabbed violently and pushed face down onto what felt like a roughly upholstered sofa. "Keep your eyes closed, and don't move." The hood was pulled off and quickly replaced with a blindfold. It was tied so tightly it was like a vise on my head, and I began to feel dizzy. Something cold and sharp was suddenly pressed threateningly against my throat. A knife? Scissors? I braced myself and told myself not to scream. I didn't want to be gagged on top of everything else that was happening to me. I held my breath in anticipation of

185

certain torture. To my surprise, no blood was let; the blade sliced through the fabric of my shirt, then was dragged repeatedly through my hoodie...my favorite hoodie...until it must have been reduced to a pile of rags on the floor. I heard one of the men laugh and mutter something under his breath. Did they just high five each other? I tried to stop myself from crying, but tears began to flow.

I sensed another person enter the room. Were there three now? I heard an air conditioner kick on, and as I felt the cool air rush across my exposed flesh, I grew quite upset about the loss of my beloved hoodie. I quickly realized I had more pressing matters at hand when I felt my shoes being yanked off and my pants violently removed. The blade wasn't used this time, but I had a feeling those jeans would never be the same again. It occurred to me I may not be either.

I jumped as I felt a sharp pain course through me, and I realized I'd been struck by a very strong hand. The hand struck me again, and once more, this time even harder. My ass was on fire. I let out a small whimper, but I tried not to cry any more. After the earlier warnings to remain quiet, I had a feeling that being witnessed crying might yield extremely undesirable results. I couldn't have been more wrong.

"Oh, she thinks she's a tough one," one of the men said with a laugh. "I guess we need to teach her a lesson." His hand made violent contact with my ass again and again, in exactly the same spot, until I thought I couldn't possibly bear any more. He stopped, and I heard heavy footsteps as he walked across the room. "Your turn, my hand hurts," he muttered with another laugh. Seconds later, I felt a smaller hand brush across what had to be the biggest welt an ass had ever experienced. The hand felt icy cold, and I had to stifle a sigh at the tiny amount of relief it provided. That relief was regrettably short-lived. The hand began to slap my other ass cheek, far too many times for me to count. He wasn't as strong as his cohort. Be thankful for small mercies, I thought to myself sardonically as my brain began to completely shut down. Nothing hurt any more, and I felt myself almost floating outside my body. It was much better there, where I couldn't feel the stings of that strange, tireless hand.

My mind was propelled back into my body by the sound of whispering across the room. I couldn't make out

187

the words. The hand that had been destroying my ass was suddenly grasping my hair and yanking my head back. I heard the sound of a zipper and then two men laughing. "Open your mouth, Bitch." My head was pulled back even more, and I felt a cock forcing itself against my lips. "Now! Or do you want another beating?" I opened my mouth and instantly gagged as the cock thrust mercilessly against the back of my throat. Tears streamed down my cheeks as I tried my very hardest not to vomit. The cock slammed into my mouth over and over, with harder and harder thrusts. "That's right. Take it, Whore." I didn't think I could take another second. He finally eased up, and just as I thought I would surely pass out from lack of oxygen, I was able to catch my breath. I heard another zipper unzipping, and two hands yanked my hips up off the sofa. My panties were unceremoniously torn from my body, and a cock pushed roughly against my ass. I jumped as it brushed painfully across the welts. "Keep still. Don't you dare move again."

The cock shoved its way into my ass, and I made an effort to remain still despite the searing pain. The other man continued to fuck my mouth, and as they plunged into me in unison, I began to leave my body once again. The pain was miraculously transformed from unbearable to almost indiscernible. Everything was suddenly wonderfully numb as the men continued to pound into me for what seemed like an eternity. I was lamentably roused from this nearly blissful state by two hands viciously grasping my ass cheeks, right on the welts. I shrieked loudly, unable to obey the repeated warnings to remain silent. Despite my anesthetized state, the pain was worse than anything I had ever imagined. With a cock still in my mouth and another ramming mercilessly into my ass, I passed out.

I awoke, having no idea how much time had gone by. I was still blindfolded, and I realized I had been left on the sofa, but I felt warmer. I was still naked, but I was covered with something. A blanket, perhaps? I felt disoriented, and I trembled beneath the blanket as the pain began to fully hit me once again. I realized my hands were no longer tied, but I was afraid to move, not sure who might be in the room and what was in store for me. I lay there as still as possible until I felt a hand brush across my face, and I instinctively backed away from it. To my surprise, the hand stroked my cheek softly, then grasped the top of the blindfold, slipping it up over my head.

It took me a while to adjust to the light in the room, but I finally made out a face in front of mine. "That was amazing," my boyfriend whispered, reaching out to gently stroke my hair. "Thank you so much for suggesting it."

Marked

Jessica lay silently on her stomach in the posh hotel room Owen had reserved for their anniversary weekend. They'd shared an amazing dinner of crab cakes and blackened redfish, with beignets for dessert. She was full and drowsy, and the ridiculously comfortable mattress was drawing her closer and closer to sleep. As she began to drift off, Owen entered the room with a large black bag. She smiled lazily at him, and he smiled back and tossed the bag onto the bed. "Time to get up, Sleepyhead," he said with a wicked grin, and despite her state of languor, she immediately rose from the bed and stood naked and awaiting further instructions. "Put this on the bed." He handed her a black blanket which was water resistant on one side and silky smooth on the other. Jessica spread it across the bed, making sure the entire surface was covered. Goosebumps formed on her arms as she smoothed the blanket down and pondered what might be in store that required such preparations.

191

"Come over here and turn around," Owen ordered her gently, and she walked towards him, turning to face away from him as soon as she reached him. She wanted to throw her arms around him, to embrace him and profess her love, but instead she stood silently, her back to him, and waited. Owen placed his hands at the back of her neck, unbuckling the simple leather collar she'd been wearing for so long that it felt odd whenever she didn't have it on. "I thought you deserved something that suits you a bit better," he said as he removed the collar from her neck. He reached over her head and placed a thick stainless steel collar around her throat. He closed the hinge carefully, making sure not to pinch her, and he sighed in relief as he discovered it was a perfect fit. He took a tiny screw and an allen wrench from the bag and locked the collar shut. "You'll need to ask me to unlock it if you need to take it off. Since you hate traveling by plane, you shouldn't have any reason to remove it." He grasped her shoulders and spun her around to face him, and they both smiled widely at each other.

Jessica's hands rose up to feel the smooth metal band, and she was overcome with joy. It was just a symbol, but it was a powerful one, and she fought the urge to run to the mirror and admire her new collar. They'd been with each other for two years now, and she'd accepted his collar a little over a year ago. She'd worn it with pride, but she was so happy to have this more enduring symbol of their bond. She felt completely on top of the world, and she had never been happier than she was in this moment.

"It's perfect on you. Now sit on the bed, I'm not quite done with our anniversary celebration." Jessica took a seat on the edge of the bed, and Owen slipped a leather blindfold over her head. She smiled, knowing something wonderful always followed when he used the blindfold on her. "I'm not binding your hands or feet this time, but I want you to lie on your stomach and remain totally still. Don't move a muscle." Jessica nodded and scooted up onto the bed, positioning herself face down directly in the center of the mattress. She breathed in the pleasant aroma of the leather blindfold, and she smiled to herself as she reflected on what a wonderful day it has been thus far. She couldn't wait to see what came next.

Jessica heard him walk across the room, and a few moments later she felt him sit down next to her and felt his hands caressing her shoulders, back, and ass. "I'm going to mark you as mine," he whispered as he ran his hands through her thick hair, pulling it to the side to reveal the blank canvas of her back. "Let me know if this is too much for you, but you're such a good girl, I'm pretty sure you can handle it."

Jessica drew in a deep breath as she felt a cold, sharp metal object glide across her shoulder. It almost tickled, then suddenly the tickle became a burning, surprising sensation as the blade penetrated her skin. She felt it cutting into her, and the blade paused, then curved to the left. The pain began to fully register, and she gasped audibly. He stopped briefly, massaging her with his free hand and giving her a chance to protest. When she didn't, he continued. Jessica had wondered for a while what it would feel like to be cut; she'd never had a tattoo, and she was always embarrassed to admit to her kinky friends that she panicked whenever she had to get a shot or have blood drawn. She could handle hours of flogging, but this had always been the one thing that engendered in her a rather equal measure of curiosity and terror. She took another deep breath then relaxed her body until she began to melt into the plush mattress. She was well versed in the art of handling pain, and she knew she could endure this.

Owen set the blade down as he completed the first phase of his design. He sat for a moment and watched the small trickles of blood merge and form a large red mass. He found it intoxicating, and he briefly considered abandoning his project in favor of tasting her blood, rubbing his body against her reddened back, and fucking her in the most animal of ways. He persuaded himself to shake off those urges, at least for a while, and he returned to his task. He picked the scalpel up off the bed and determined the perfect spot to break flesh. Jessica cried out as the blade again pierced her skin. He realized the blade had gone a bit too deep when the blood began to flow a bit too freely, so he eased up and lightened the pressure against her back. He completed the lines almost too quickly, and decided to slow down and savor the rest of his task.

Jessica felt as if every nerve ending in her body had migrated to that one small spot on her back. She felt on fire, and the gliding of the blade created such acute pain that she almost couldn't fathom taking any more. She continued to breathe, and to think about how pleased Owen must be at her ability to withstand this experience which she'd been so afraid of for so long. He'd spoken often of wanting to pierce her flesh, to feel and taste her blood, to

195

mark her again and again in the same place until the scars became permanent. It was exhilarating and frightening to think this was the first of many such markings.

Owen stopped to dab away the blood with a tissue, then he set back to his task. Penetrating Jessica with the scalpel turned him on beyond his wildest imaginings, and he found himself fighting harder and harder to maintain the self-control he knew he must hang onto. He ran his hand gently across the cuts he'd already made, and he smiled as he felt her shudder beneath him. He could sense her inching closer and closer to bliss, and he knew it would be amazing. He held his hand up to his face and licked the blood from it, then set about completing his work.

Jessica began to breathe more heavily as she felt the blade cutting into her and opening her up. She could tell Owen was growing more confident in his strokes, and they were coming more quickly and consistently. He obviously wanted to make sure the marks lasted a long while, because she could feel that he was retracing over the wounds he'd already inflicted. It was like nothing she'd ever experienced, searing pain consuming already slashed flesh. Her eyes fluttered beneath the blindfold, she let out a long, deep sigh, and everything began to feel soft and beautiful. As she drifted off to her happy place, the mattress felt like a cloud, and the blade's sharp stings became gentle caresses.

Owen felt Jessica's body relax and fully give in beneath him, and he redoubled his efforts to complete his work. He dragged the blade carefully over each cut once, then again, no longer stopping to dab away the excess blood. He didn't want to rush, but he knew his desire to penetrate her with more than just a scalpel blade would soon overtake him. He made one last stroke, drawing it out slowly and fully appreciating the lovely way her skin parted and reddened beneath the blade. Satisfied with his handiwork, he set the scalpel down and began to rub Jessica's back and legs. She almost seemed as though she was sleeping, but he knew she was awake, and he knew she'd be roused back to full consciousness soon enough.

Jessica felt Owen's hands caressing her, and she felt a dull throbbing sensation where he'd left his mark. It felt warm and sweet and wet. She smiled and turned her head to the side, as if attempting to look at him through the blindfold. She felt his hands on her grow more urgent, and then the blindfold was torn off, and she could see in his eyes that the self-control he'd so carefully held onto was all but gone.

Owen looked down at the blood pooling on Jessica's back, and he could restrain himself no longer. He lowered his face to her flesh and began to lap up the blood almost ferociously. He let out a bit of a growl as he ran his hands over the blood he'd missed. He grasped her shoulders and pushed her down into the mattress, then sank his teeth into an untouched area of skin, biting into her harder than he'd ever done before. He barely broke the skin, but she let out a loud moan, then a scream. He bit into her again and again, feeling more animal than human, and liking it. It had been so difficult being calm and careful as he wielded the scalpel. Now it was time to go wild.

Jessica screamed out again and again as she felt Owen's teeth tear into her. It felt so different than the careful, sharp sting of the scalpel. This was rough, violent, and amazing. She reached back and dragged her nails down his thighs as he bit into her again. The pain was so intense that she almost couldn't breathe, and her pussy was wetter than it had ever been. With her left hand still on his thigh, she pulled her right hand back and slipped it

underneath her. "May I?" she asked between moans.
Owen grunted a reply that sounded like consent, so she slid
her hand down to her drenched pussy and began to rub her
clit feverishly. The combination of pleasure and pain sent
her over the edge almost instantly, and she screamed out as
she came violently.

Owen felt Jessica's body undulate violently beneath
her, and he could wait no longer. He gave his cock a few
strokes, and he looked down with a smile as he saw the
blood from his hand staining his flesh. He released his grip
long enough to grasp Jessica's hips and pull her onto her
knees, then he sank his cock into her effortlessly, marveling
at how incredibly wet she was. He felt her hand still
rubbing her clit as he fucked her, and he moaned loudly as
he felt her pussy clench down on him with every orgasm.
He admired his handiwork as he thrust into her; the cuts
were bright red and looked beautiful on her left shoulder,
and her right shoulder was a mottled mess of bite marks
and random patches of blood. He smiled as he pondered
the lovely shades of black, blue, and purple she would be
sporting the next day. He felt her body tense up and her
breathing grow very steady, then she screamed out louder
than any amount of pain that night had caused her to

scream. Her entire body shook fiercely, and her pussy seemed to almost vibrate with the intensity of her orgasm. Owen thrust into her as hard as he could, stopped to let her pussy squeeze him again and again, then exploded inside her. Completely sated, he released her and lay next to her, stroking her hair as he slowly regained his ability to breathe.

Jessica knew Owen would sleep for a while, but she couldn't possibly wait to see her back, to see the marks he'd given her. She asked permission to get up, and he nodded with a closed-eyed smile. She ran to the bathroom and first stopped to admire her beautiful steel collar. It was the one she'd wanted for so long, but she'd never said a word to him, or to anyone else, about it. She smiled as she reflected on how well he knew her, and how much he always seemed to anticipate her needs and wants. She turned around, her back to the mirror, and looked back at the mirror to get a good view of her shoulders. She let out a small giggle at the mess her right shoulder was. She'd always loved being bitten, and he'd certainly taken it to a new level tonight. Her eyes then moved to her left shoulder, and she smiled at the beautiful simplicity of what he'd placed on her back, what he assured her he would make permanent: "Owen's."

Indeed, she was his. Permanently.

The Gift

     Phillip tapped his foot nervously on the elevator ride up to the 14th floor. He was normally rather nonchalant, but he found himself suddenly rather terrified of what might be transpiring once they reached the hotel suite. His mistress had made it very clear that her birthday plan was to serve him up to various friends on a metaphorical silver platter, though, and he would willingly oblige. He'd been with Courtney for years, so long that he hardly remembered being physical with another woman.

     Phillip and Courtney had been monogamous since their first date, and they'd gotten serious quickly. When her dominant tendencies surfaced, he was quietly thrilled. He'd never felt like the one in charge in their relationship, and he'd often worried something was wrong with him, and that as soon as she discovered his shortcomings, she'd leave him. He'd joyfully served her every whim for over five years. In all that time, she'd never even hinted at their playing with anyone else. They went to parties where she beat him mercilessly in front of a crowd of admiring onlookers. They'd had sex in front of the same people, but they'd never invited anyone to join them. The turn-on for her had always been in the exhibitionism. She said she enjoyed showing him off to others. He had always prided himself in his body, and in his commitment to work out five days a week no matter how hectic life became. He didn't act like a jerk about it, but he knew he looked good, and he enjoyed it when she put him on display for their friends and acquaintances.

This, however, was so different. She hadn't even told him what would be expected. Sex? Beatings? Both? She'd simply said to be ready for whatever might happen. What a way to make someone nervous! He knew Courtney had a sadistic streak not only when it came to the physical side of things, but also the mental. She was fucking with him, and she was enjoying it. All he could do was take a few deep breaths and tell himself it would all be okay. Hell, perhaps it might even be fun. A small touch of guilt arose in him when he pondered that possibility. Was he *supposed* to enjoy this? Would that even be acceptable to her? He assumed he'd find out soon enough. The elevator finally opened, and she led him to their suite.

Phillip entered the room and looked around with a smile. Courtney had clearly spent some time preparing things. Candles were placed around the room, already lit, rope was tied to the bedposts, and an assortment of riding crops, floggers, and other implements rested on the loveseat next to the bed. Yes, this would be quite the party.

"Did you take a shower before I picked you up?" Courtney asked, looking him over carefully. "Yes, of course I did," Phillip replied with a slight roll of his eyes. She swatted his ass playfully. "No need to get snarky, Phillip. Take off your clothes and lie down on the bed." Phillip obeyed at once, pulling his shirt over his head and slipping his shoes and jeans off. He climbed onto the bed and lay on his side, resting his head on his arm and smiling cheekily at his mistress. "Okay, Smartass. You're not here for a photo shoot. On your back. *Now.*" She gave him another swat, and he lay on his back, his head sinking into the comfy goose down pillow.

Courtney wasted no time in using the rope on the bedposts to secure his wrists. He had just enough slack to avoid arm strain, and to sit up if so ordered. Courtney knew Phillip well enough to know he wouldn't take advantage of that small mercy. He lay back, gently tugged the ropes to make sure they were secure, then asked if she would be blindfolding him before their little adventure. "Oh, absolutely *not*," she replied with a wicked smile. "I want you to be able to see *everything*." She let out a slightly foreboding laugh, then she walked to the French doors separating the bedroom of the suite from the sitting area. She opened the doors, and Phillip's eyes grew wide.

He could see at least four people sitting on the posh sofa, and another leaning against the wall. Two of the guests were extremely attractive women, one of whom was Courtney's close friend and a fellow domme, and another he'd never seen before. There were also three men he didn't recognize. Phillip did a double take as this registered in his overwhelmed brain. Why were there *men* here for the party? Perhaps Courtney didn't want him having all the fun. Understandable. And Phillip had secretly longed to watch Courtney fuck another man. But three? That might be overdoing it just a tad, even for her birthday! Phillip stifled a laugh as he imagined Courtney finding herself deluged with men, all wanting a part of her, while she attempted to control what her female friends did to her sub. This was going to be an interesting night, without a doubt.

Courtney entered the sitting area and spoke in a muffled voice to her party guests. Phillip felt his cock stir in anticipation of being teased, beaten, sucked and fucked. Happy birthday to Courtney, indeed! His nerves were all but settled, and he was ready for an experience like none he'd ever had. He smiled broadly as Courtney's friend Gemma approached the bed. She was wearing a leather corset and tight, dark blue jeans. He silently hoped she'd be removing those jeans very, very soon.

Gemma walked over to the spread of toys on the loveseat, and she picked up and examined each one. She settled on a simple black crop, and she flipped it over in her hands a few times, finally nodding and turning her attention to Phillip. Courtney was nowhere to be seen, which gave Phillip pause until the sharp sting of the crop on his upper thigh commanded his full attention. He let out an embarrassingly high pitched squeal, and Gemma laughed loudly. "*Really*, Phillip? Courtney led me to believe you were more of a man than *that*. Buck up, it's gonna be a long night." She struck him with the crop several more times, gently caressing his thigh once she was done. She focused on his other thigh now, striking even harder, but Phillip was determined not to make a sound this time. His breathing grew heavier, and Gemma smiled, knowing he was either really enjoying it, or really hating it. She was good with either one.

After a few more minutes with the crop, Gemma tossed it to the side of the bed and produced a Wartenburg pinwheel from her back pocket. Wow, Phillip mused, she really came prepared! She smiled a somewhat malicious grin, crawled onto him, and ran the pinwheel over his stomach and chest. After a while, she began to use more force, and Phillip found himself panting as the tiny steel pins pressed into his flesh. He blushed as he realized he'd grown fully erect and his cock was pressing forcefully into Gemma's thigh. "Do you want to fuck me?" Gemma asked him with a coy smile as she noticed it too. "Yes, please," Phillip replied with a sigh of relief, quite anxious for her to tear those jeans off.

"Well, you're out of luck, Sweetness. I don't fuck my friends' subs. It's unbecoming." She giggled at his look of utter dejection, and she glanced down at his erection and laughed again, just to add a little punch to her denial. She adjusted her position and straddled him roughly, pressing herself down against his rigid cock. She clearly enjoyed the tease. When he let out a soft whimper, she rolled the pinwheel across his chest so hard he was certain she'd break his skin. She inched closer and closer to his nipples, then circled them twice, pressing so hard he couldn't stifle himself any longer, and he began to moan loudly. He had always loved pain, and lots of it, and he was in heaven.

Phillip noticed Courtney enter the room with a muscular, tan guy with dark brown, wavy hair and a trimmed beard. Even in Phillip's state of near-bliss, he paused to contemplate how peculiar it was that Courtney had chosen this man to fuck. He wasn't at all her type. He knew he'd thoroughly enjoy the show regardless, and he felt his cock grow even harder at the thought of what was to come. As Gemma continued to roll the pinwheel over his flesh, he smiled and waited for the show to begin.

"This is Travis," Courtney stated rather matter-of-factly as a wicked smirk began to spread across her face. Travis began to undress, and Courtney stood near the foot of the bed, her attention divided between watching him undress and observing Gemma work her magic with the pinwheel. Phillip couldn't help noticing that Courtney was remaining fully clothed. He began to grow a bit impatient, as he'd secretly fantasized about this moment for so long. He was roused from his thoughts by a cock suddenly poised centimeters from his face. He jumped involuntarily in surprise, and both Courtney and Gemma laughed loudly. "Open your mouth, Silly," Courtney commanded Phillip, rolling her eyes.

Phillip's mind began to race. He'd never sucked cock in his life. Honestly, he'd never even *considered* it. He had gay friends, sure, but he'd never had any interest in men beyond basic friendship. What happened to his fantasy of seeing this muscle bound guy fuck Courtney? What in the hell was going on? Amidst these rapidly occurring thoughts, he looked at Courtney with a pleading expression on his face. Courtney was no longer smiling. She walked closer to him and slapped him hard across his hip. "Suck his cock, Phillip. *Now*."

Phillip closed his eyes and opened his mouth, and Travis forced his cock all the way to the back of Phillip's throat. Phillip gagged, and Travis eased up a bit, then began to thrust into him gently. Phillip opened his eyes and saw Travis grasping his cock at the base as he thrust. Phillip began to try harder to take it all, and he moved his head forward, towards Travis, and took his cock as deeply as possible into his mouth. Travis began to moan as he pushed himself into Phillip's mouth, and Phillip found himself shockingly aroused. The combination of this unexpected turn of events, combined with Gemma's now-gentler use of the pinwheel on him, had him hard as a rock and feeling like he might burst at any moment.

Just as Phillip found himself really getting into the first blow job he'd ever performed, Travis let out a loud, guttural moan, pulled out, and came all over Phillip's face. Travis continued stroking his cock until every last drop had been expelled, then he bent down to retrieve his clothes, pulled his jeans on, and left the room. Gemma followed suit, returning the pinwheel to her pocket and exiting without so much as a goodbye. Phillip suddenly felt more self-conscious than he'd ever felt before. He licked his lips furtively, noting with surprise that the taste wasn't bad at all. He was glad, though, that he hadn't had to take it all in his mouth.

Courtney approached Phillip with a warm, damp towel and gently cleaned his face. "Such a good boy you're being for my birthday. I almost thought you were enjoying that. Perhaps it's time for a little treat." She left momentarily, returning with the other woman he'd seen lounging in the sitting room. She'd stripped down to a lace bra and panties, and she was absolutely stunning. Piercing blue eyes, black hair cut into a short bob, and skin so pale it looked as though she hadn't been in the sun for years. She glanced at Courtney, who gave her a silent nod, then she climbed onto Phillip, crawling seductively until she was kneeling over his chest. He let out a sigh, savoring the anticipation of what might come next.

The woman arched her back and caressed her breasts seductively. Phillip wished he was untied so he could touch her gorgeous, lily white skin. He ached to run his hands along her sides, down her hips, to slide his fingers underneath those lace panties. As he was pondering that thought, she slowly slithered up his chest until she was straddling his face. She yanked her panties to the side and lowered her pussy onto his eager mouth. More aroused than he thought possible, he began to lap at her clit hungrily. She moaned, grinding her pussy onto his face

211

and slamming her hands against the headboard. She moved her hips forward a bit, and his tongue began plunging feverishly into her pussy. Her moans grew louder and louder, and she slid back down so he could tongue her clit again. Her entire body shuddered, but she didn't stop forcing her pussy down onto his face. She wanted more, and she was going to get it.

Phillip hadn't noticed anyone else enter the room, but he suddenly felt a hand on his ever-hardening cock. The hand stroked him as he continued to lick and suck at the clit poised over his mouth. The hand on his cock was soon replaced with a mouth, and Phillip let out a growl as waves of pleasure immediately began coursing through his body. Whoever was sucking his cock possessed extreme skill and was taking his entire cock with each stroke, with just the right amount of suction. He gasped, and his body jerked, almost tossing the woman off of him. He forced himself to remain still and to finish her off, and as he ran his tongue across her clit forcefully, she let out a scream, held herself down against his tongue as her entire body shook, then climbed off him and collapsed onto the loveseat next to the bed.

Phillip was finally able to catch his breath, and to look down to see who was sucking him so expertly. It was a thin, extremely attractive boy who looked like he was in his early twenties. Despite what had already transpired, the taboo nature of being sucked off by a hot young guy took him by surprise and excited him tremendously. He watched the boy's mouth slide up and down his shaft, and he noticed how skillfully he paused and swirled his tongue around the tip of Phillips cock. Phillip began to breathe heavily, and he knew he was about to explode into the boy's mouth. "No, you don't!" Courtney commanded him with a firm slap, and he focused all his energy on not coming. Courtney smiled and patted him on the chest. "That's a good boy," she praised him as he grimaced from his efforts to maintain self-control. After a few more minutes, Courtney patted the boy on his shoulder, and he rose from the bed and exited the room. Phillip realized the woman had left as well; he'd been so caught up with one of the best blow jobs he'd ever received that he didn't even notice her leave.

"Are you enjoying my birthday?" Courtney asked with a sly smile. Finding himself unable to form words, Phillip nodded enthusiastically. Courtney sat next to him and rubbed his arm. "My original plan was to line up a few people to beat you. But I decided this would be more fun. For us both." She smiled again, glancing behind her at the sitting room and nodding before returning her gaze to Phillip. One more to go. This is going to be a good one, so get ready!" Phillip gulped audibly, and she laughed again.

This time, Courtney began removing her dress and kicking her shoes off. Phillip watched her undress, enjoying the view as he always did. His mistress was absolutely beautiful, and he never tired of examining the curves of her body. He was so caught up in admiring her that he didn't realize a third man had appeared. This one was more Courtney's type. Tall, slender, not by any means a gym rat, but he clearly took care of himself. He had a dark brown mop of hair and brown eyes which seemed to glisten as he smiled at them both. "I'm Justin," he said to Phillip with a small nod. Courtney scooted next to Phillip on the bed, and he held his breath, waiting to see what would come next. He'd dreamed of enjoying her body along with another man, but he knew better than to assume *anything* after the evening's events thus far.

Courtney kissed Phillip deeply as Justin stood near the foot of the bed, seeming to admire them both. Phillip closed his eyes and surrendered to her kiss, realizing that this was the first time today he'd actually kissed her. His head had been swimming with thoughts, but for a moment, his mind went blank as he melted into her, feeling a closeness he'd never quite felt before. Justin crawled onto the bed and sat near them, but he didn't touch them. They kissed a bit longer, and Courtney caressed Phillip's chest, abdomen, and thighs before encircling his cock with her soft hand. "I've been thinking about this moment for so long, Phillip. You trust me, right?" Phillip nodded enthusiastically, dizzy with adoration for her.

Courtney reached over to the night table and grabbed a bottle of lube. She poured some onto her hand and again slipped down to his cock, giving it a few lingering strokes before she continued on to his ass. She slipped a lubed finger into his ass and he let out a sigh. He'd always enjoyed that, and he held his breath, waiting for a second finger. As he anticipated, she removed her finger and then entered him with two. He moaned at the feeling of pressure, at the lovely intensity of it. She pushed into him gently, then more forcefully, and he felt his cock stand at attention. His head fell to the side and he growled softly into his shoulder as she began to thrust her fingers into him quicker and quicker. He started to shudder and she immediately pulled away. She smiled as he let out a disappointed whimper.

Phillip opened his eyes and saw Justin slipping a condom on, then lubing himself up. Courtney watched admiringly, then returned her attention to Phillip, stroking his cock slowly but firmly. Justin moved closer, placing his hands on Phillip's legs and pulling them up off the mattress. He rubbed Phillip's thigh with one hand while the other hand found his ass and slipped a finger in just as Courtney had done. For the third time that night, Phillip gasped as he found himself experiencing something he'd never imagined. Justin removed his finger, then rubbed Phillip's ass for a moment before gently thrusting his cock into it.

Phillip's hips rose off the bed, and he let out a loud, sharp moan. Courtney quickened the pace of her hand on his cock, and he settled back down onto the bed, trying his hardest to relax. As he did, the sensation of being penetrated by a cock for the first time became less and less painful, and then began to feel incredibly pleasurable. Justin noticed Phillip's sighs of pleasure, and he plunged his cock into him harder as he watched Courtney's hand skillfully working Phillip over. Both Phillip and Justin began to moan loudly, almost in unison, as the pleasure built, and when Justin came with one final violent thrust inside Phillip's ass, Phillip exploded into Courtney's hand and onto Justin's stomach.

Justin headed for the bathroom to clean up, and Courtney followed him. She returned with another wet towel and wiped Phillip's cock clean. She tossed the towel aside and untied him, happy to allow him to put his arms around her and hold her for the first time that night. Phillip did just that, holding her tightly and whimpering softly against her chest. She rubbed his back, then she ran her fingers softly through his hair. "Thank you," she whispered as he clung to her. "I knew you'd happily let anyone I brought here beat you. I wanted to see you REALLY submit to me. And you did. You made this the best birthday ever." She kissed him softly on the cheek and lips as he drifted off to sleep.

Couple Seeks Single Male:

Swinging Encounters Book One

By

Audra Morgan

Couple Seeks Single Male: Swinging Encounters Book One

Copyright © 2012 by Audra Morgan

Audra can be contacted by email at

AudraMorganBooks@gmail.com

The First Time

"I don't know what to wear!" Katie shouted from the bathroom as Joe put his shoes on in the foyer. "What difference does it make?" He replied with a chuckle. "It's not going to be on you very long anyway!" He turned around to see Katie standing behind him, not looking even a little amused. "Shut Up! I'm nervous!" She retorted, practically wringing her hands with worry. "Nervous? *You're* nervous?!" Joe couldn't help laughing again, thinking that surely he must be a thousand times *more* nervous than Katie. He'd been vacillating all afternoon between being really excited and wanting to call the whole thing off.

But they'd met Matt the week before for drinks, and they'd had a great time. The conversation flowed effortlessly, they found themselves laughing almost nonstop, and by the end of the night they felt like old friends. Mass quantities of tequila tend to do that. But it was more than the tequila. He was a really cool guy, someone they liked as a person, and someone they both felt would be a good candidate for their first foray into this new territory. He'd never done this before either, and fortunately, he seemed to feel the same affinity towards Katie and Joe. So here they were, walking out the door on their way to a new experience, hoping it would go well, and knowing that whatever might happen that night, they'd have an amazing time together when they returned home.

They met up at the same bar from the week before – a little hole-in-the-wall place Matt had suggested. It was casual and cozy, and the drinks were strong. Perfect! When they arrived, Matt was already waiting for them at the bar. They settled into a table in the corner, away from the juke box, and they ordered drinks and caught up on the events of the past week. They drank and laughed and grew a bit less nervous, but they were all still a little anxious about the events to come. Katie sat nervously between Joe and Matt, not sure if she should be flirting with Matt or playing it cool. She felt like a kid in first grade with a crush on a boy in her class. She didn't know the rules, and she didn't want to look foolish or make anyone angry. She breathed a sigh of relief when Matt casually placed his hand on her knee as he relayed a funny story about a coworker. Joe looked down to see Matt's hand on Katie's leg, and he smiled at her, and she suddenly felt much better.

After an hour of drinks, conversation, and waves of nervousness, Matt asked if they'd like to head to his apartment. Katie and Joe nodded, downed the remainder of their cocktails, and walked together to the parking lot. Joe told Matt he'd follow him to his place, since they'd never been there before. They made the short drive to Matt's house, nervously laughing the whole way. "You sure about this?" Joe asked, squeezing Katie's hand. "Ummmm...I think so," she replied with a nervous sigh. They pulled up in front of a small duplex, and Katie knew they were past the point of no return. She'd been the one who had originally told Joe she wanted to try a threesome with another man. They'd had threesomes with women before, and it had always been pretty fun. But she wondered what it would be like to be with two men, and after months of talking about it, looking online for men they might want to meet, and finally agreeing on Matt, here they were. Katie was nervous, excited, and finally felt like she was ready to make it happen.

Matt unlocked the front door and held it open as they entered. They all stood in the living room, each of them awkwardly pondering how to move things along. Finally, Joe suggested they move things to the bedroom. He put his

222

arm around Katie, reassuring her, and they walked together down the short hallway into Matt's room. Joe gently pushed Katie in Matt's direction, and she realized that the talkative, confident guy from the bar had become quite shy and reserved. For some reason, this made Katie feel more comfortable. Joe gave her another nudge, and she moved towards Matt and kissed him. Her nerves subsided as she felt Joe's hands gliding along her back and down her sides, and he positioned himself closer against her and kissed the back of her neck.

Katie began to kiss Matt more deeply, circling his neck with her hands and running her fingers through his hair. He let out a soft moan, and as she pressed herself closer to him, she could feel his cock straining against his jeans. With Joe kissing her neck and rubbing her back, she began to explore Matt's body as she kissed him, running her hands down the front of his chest, to his stomach, and over the bulge in his jeans. His breathing grew heavier, and he pulled her closer and kissed her hard.

Katie realized this really wasn't all that different from any other threesome they'd had in the past, despite the obvious gender difference of their companion. They were together, enjoying a new experience, and we were having fun so far. She realized she couldn't just sit back this time, though, like she'd been able to do when they were with women; this was most definitely all about her. She lifted her arms up as she felt Joe pulling her top up and sliding it over her head. Matt's hands found her breasts and rubbed them gently, then gave her nipples a little pinch. She gasped as the sensation hit her, and her breathing quickened. She felt Joe's hands slipping her skirt down, then her panties, and she stood naked between them. Suddenly hands were all over her, and any shyness or uncertainty was gone. Joe's hands rubbed her ass, then slid around her hips and began to explore her pussy. He smiled and kissed her ear as he discovered she was already quite wet. Matt quickly removed his clothes and returned to his position in front of Katie. He pressed himself close to her, reveling in the softness of her skin against his. Joe took a seat on the bed and undressed as he watched his wife kissing and touching Matt. He suggested they join him on the bed, and they did.

Katie had a sudden flash of worry; she wasn't sure what she was supposed to be doing, and how she would please both men. Much to her relief, Joe immediately guided her to the middle of the bed and positioned himself to her right, and Matt lay to her left, and they both began kissing her, touching her, enjoying her body. It was so much more comfortable than she had expected, and she just lay there and enjoyed the feel of being surrounded by eager, skilled hands and mouths. After several minutes of near bliss, Joe placed his hand on Katie's shoulder and guided her down towards Matt's cock, and as she began to suck him, Joe slid his hands between her legs and rubbed her clit in just the way he knew she liked. Joe watched her intently as she sucked Matt's cock, and from the look in his eyes, it was clear to Katie that he approved. He'd never gotten to see her with another man, and the view was extraordinarily arousing.

Katie continued working Matt's cock with her mouth, taking it all and enjoying his moans and the way he gasped every time his cock hit the back of her throat. Joe's hand on her pussy was almost distracting, but as she sucked Matt, she could feel herself getting wetter and wetter, and she had to stop a few times to catch her breath. As Joe began to rub her with more force, Katie felt her entire body shudder, and she was overcome by an orgasm that rivaled any she'd ever had before. She let her mouth slip off

Matt's cock, and she lay there for a moment, reeling from the pleasure coursing through her body. Matt caressed her breasts and stomach as she lay there panting, then he pushed her towards Joe, who clearly needed some attention. Katie slipped her lips onto his remarkably hard cock as he knelt over her. She was so focused on licking and sucking her husband's cock that she was caught by surprise when she felt Matt between her legs. He lapped hungrily at her clit as he gently slipped a finger into her, and waves of pleasure again began to course through her body. She continued to kiss and suck and lick Joe's cock as she enjoyed Matt's mouth and tongue and fingers, and she was hardly able to contain her utter surprise at how amazing it felt. She came again, shuddering violently with Joe's cock still in her mouth.

Katie was dizzy with pleasure, and she collapsed back onto the bed, not sure who would be fucking her first. She was ready to feel a cock pounding into her pussy, and she didn't know which one she wanted first. As she pondered this, she noticed Joe give Matt a little nod. She watched as Joe lay back down on the bed, turned her over onto her side, and positioned himself behind her, and Matt lay down facing her. Joe suddenly bit her shoulder rather hard, and she felt his erection pressing against her ass. Marveling at the fact that he'd gotten hard again so quickly, she gasped from the sting of the bite and then from the unexpected feeling of his cock suddenly plunging into her ass. She let out a loud moan as she relished the sensation of him forcing himself into her tight ass; it wasn't something they did often, but she always enjoyed it, and she knew he did too. Matt kissed her very gently and cradled her face in his hand, then he began to rub his cock against her pussy. She felt it against her clit and sighed deeply, enjoying the teasing little caresses as he kissed her and Joe fucked her ass.

She began to quiver, feeling as though she might come again just from his cock rubbing against her. He suddenly pulled away just a bit, then slipped his cock into her pussy, forcefully pushing himself all the way into her. Katie let out a scream from the shock of this new sensation. She'd never felt anything like it before, and it was so intense she almost couldn't breathe. At first, Joe paced his thrusts so that as he pushed into her, Matt pulled out, and she began to get used to the feeling and the rhythm of it, and it felt amazing. After a while, Joe began to thrust into her at the same time Matt did, and Katie thought she'd pass out. It was painful and amazing, being completely filled up like that, and she held her breath in a vain attempt to keep from screaming. The sensations were almost too much to bear, but it was also the most incredible thing she'd ever felt. She felt Matt's cock swell even more inside her as he came with a loud moan. Just as he pulled out, Joe exploded inside her and then collapsed face-first onto the bed. It took everyone several minutes to regain their ability to speak, walk, or do anything else. Katie lay there, utterly spent, covered in sweat, and smiling from ear to ear. It had been everything she'd dreamed of, and she was perfectly happy.

Realizing the time, Joe said they had to get going. They got dressed, she hugged Matt goodbye, and they walked to the door. "Free next weekend?" Joe asked Matt with a laugh before they headed to their car. Matt nodded and told Joe to text him any time. Katie smiled widely, excited about what new adventures the next weekend might hold.

The Woman at the Bar

Jacob walked into the Crescent Moon Pub and looked around, surprised at how crowded it was for a Wednesday night. He noticed that a good bit of people had their eyes on the numerous flat screen televisions mounted on the walls, and he realized there was a game on. He didn't keep up with sports much, so he never knew when some championship game or other might bring a crowd to the bars. After looking around a bit, he focused his attention on the main bar, and he immediately noticed a tall, thin brunette wearing a short floral dress. "Bingo," he thought to himself as he approached her slowly.

The woman was sipping a tequila sunrise and looking nervously around the room. She appeared to be standing there alone, although there were groups of people on either side of her, all of whom were focused intently on the televisions. Ambient bar chatter was interrupted by a loud chorus of cheers from most of the crowd, but the woman continued to work on her drink, not even glancing up at the television screen. Jacob saw her face when she looked over towards the side of the bar. She seemed to be about forty, and although that was nearly twice his age, she was absolutely stunning. She wore very little makeup, but her features were striking. Her skin was pale, but her cheeks had a rosy glow, and her lips were full and looked rather kissable from his vantage point. As she turned her head back to face the bar, Jacob noticed how amazing her legs looked, pale and toned and rather exposed by the short dress she wore. Her strappy sandals were sexy as hell. Jacob had a thing for a woman in cute sandals; he'd take those over stilettos any day. Jacob also couldn't help noticing the huge diamond on her left hand. Her husband must be a wealthy man, and a *lucky* man, he thought to himself with a smile.

Jacob moved forward in the woman's direction until he was standing behind her. He stood there for a moment, and she glanced back at him and then quickly turned her head forward without acknowledging him at all. He noticed her begin to twirl the straw around and around in her glass. She was clearly nervous. She picked the glass up, sucked down its contents, and motioned to the bartender for another. Her drink was quickly refilled, and she took another sip before setting the glass down and returning to her straw-twirling. Jacob shook his head when the bartender asked if he needed anything. He pretended to watch the game for a minute, but he couldn't care less about which team was winning or losing. He breathed in, enjoying the soft floral perfume the woman had generously applied. It was quite literally a breath of fresh air among a room crowded with smokers.

Jacob hesitated a moment, then slowly reached out a hand and rested it on the woman's shoulder. He felt her tense up, then he saw her release the straw she'd been using to furiously stir her drink. She set her hand on the bar and looked down at her shoes. Jacob's hand glided down her back to her hip, and he gave it a small squeeze. Her body reacted by tilting back a bit until her shoulders made brief contact with his chest. She moved forward again, appearing to be trying desperately not to turn around. Jacob smiled, although she couldn't see him, and he leaned forward until his mouth was next to her ear. "My God, you're sexy," he whispered softly as she appeared to stifle a smile and look away from him. "And you smell amazing," he added, noting that she was apparently pretending she

231

couldn't hear him. He smiled again, gave her hip another soft squeeze, then slid his hand forward until it was grasping her upper thigh.

The woman leaned forward against the bar and picked up her drink, taking a quick sip before putting the glass down and resting both hands on the edge of the bar. Jacob closed the gap she'd created by moving forward a bit, and he placed his left hand on her waist as his right hand continued exploring her thigh. He could feel her body heave as she took a deep breath in, but she made no sound, and she still didn't acknowledge his presence. As she reached for her drink again, his hand traveled up her thigh until his fingers traced the lace outline of her panties. The woman gasped and nearly dropped her drink. She set it down quickly and glanced up at the television, watching a commercial for some new hybrid vehicle as she felt the hand on her thigh again make its way to her panties, this time sliding underneath them. She felt a finger slip easily inside her, and her face flushed at the realization of how wet she'd become from the attention she'd been receiving. The finger slipped back out and made circular motions around her clit, and she failed miserably at attempting to appear nonchalant.

Fortunately, the home team scored once again, and the crowd in the bar began cheering wildly. Jacob took this opportunity to press himself firmly against her and to plunge two fingers as deeply into her pussy as they'd go. She let out an audible gasp, but all eyes were on the televisions. Jacob's left hand slid from her side around to her stomach and then made its way down into her panties. He stroked her clit deftly with his left hand as his right hand continued to work its way in and out of her pussy. She was clearly exerting a great deal of effort to remain calm and still, but Jacob could feel the pressure building inside her. He kept an eye on the television, stroking her just enough to keep her wanting more as he awaited another round of cheers from the crowd. The team scored again, the crowd went wild, and Jacob began stroking her clit feverishly and forcing his fingers into her as quickly as he could. She lurched forward and let out an unintentional moan as she came violently, squirting all over his hand and all over her own legs. She closed her eyes and breathed heavily for a few moments, then when the loud merriment of her fellow bar patrons died down, she quickly regained her composure and realized she'd made a bit of a mess.

"I think we need to get you cleaned off," Jacob said softly as he smoothed her dress back down and took her hand. She looked him in the eyes for the first time, smiled, and followed him to the restroom. Relieved that this hole-in-the-wall bar had two locking restrooms instead of larger rooms with stalls, he opened the door to the first one and pulled her inside. He locked the door, then he grabbed a few paper towels and wiped her legs off. "That's better," he said before pushing her back against the wall and kissing her fiercely. Her hands remained at her sides, but she kissed him back with a level of intensity that shocked him. He pulled her dress up and yanked her panties to the side, holding them there and leaving her pussy exposed as they continued to kiss passionately. He finally unzipped his pants and thrust his erection into her roughly, smiling as she let out a loud moan, clearly not caring who might hear.

Jacob pounded into her voraciously, feeling like he couldn't get enough. She was so wet and tight he wanted to keep her pressed against the wall all night, fucking her until long after the bar closed. He pulled the top of her dress down until her breasts were exposed, and he rubbed and pinched her nipples gently as he fucked her. She began to pant and let out low moans, and he continued rubbing

234

her and teasing her nipples, then he gave them each a sharp pinch. She screamed out in pain, but her entire body shuddered, and he felt her pussy contracting on his cock. He continued working one nipple as his other hand trailed down to her clit, and he circled it gently with his thumb. The combination of sensations sent her over the edge, and her body shook as she winced and attempted to avoid screaming. Her orgasms were too much for Jacob to bear, and as her cunt squeezed down on his cock over and over, he knew he couldn't stop himself from coming. He gave her one final, hard thrust and burst inside her, feeling her body continue to clench down on him and squeeze out every last drop he had. When he was sated, he pulled away, zipping up his pants as he enjoyed the view of this gorgeous woman, her breasts and pussy still exposed as she leaned back against the restroom wall with her eyes closed, trying to catch her breath.

The woman finally opened her eyes, adjusted her panties and her dress, and blushed as she stood there in the brightly lit restroom with this boy that was probably young enough to be her son. He smiled, suddenly seeming shy after such an amazing display of bravado. "Thank you," he said, looking at her, then down at the floor. "And tell your husband thank you for me. I'm so glad I worked up the nerve to reply to his ad. I hope he enjoys hearing all about it." She smiled widely at the thought of that. "Trust me, he will. This was his biggest fantasy, and he can't wait for me to get home and tell him every last detail." She gave Jacob a quick kiss then walked out, anxious to get home to her husband for round two of a surprisingly delightful evening.

The Party

After a few celebratory cocktails, Paul and Ashley headed to their hotel room. It had been a phenomenal week. Paul had just gotten an amazing promotion, ensuring him a long tenure with his current employer at a more than generous salary. Moreover, Ashley had just sold several pieces of her artwork for a considerable price, and she was feeling on top of the world. It seemed only fitting to Paul that they celebrate their accomplishments by indulging in one of their seldom-acted-on fantasies.

Ashley and Paul had tried swinging, but it had never felt right to them. Paul really didn't find any other women attractive, nor did he have any interest in fucking them. His true enjoyment was in watching Ashley be pleasured by an attractive, talented lover. Ashley found that with most couples they met, the man just didn't have what it took to satisfy her, and she came out of the experience utterly unfulfilled. Then, one night, they were alone at a sex club on one of the few nights that single men were allowed, and a new fetish was born. Ashley garnered the attention of quite a few eligible bachelors, and Paul

237

thoroughly enjoyed every moment as he watched them pleasure her, one by one. They ended the night by making passionate love in the same bed she'd shared with three other men, and they found they felt closer than ever before.

So here they were, attempting to re-create that amazing night, but with a bit more planning on Paul's part. He'd carefully selected the participants, wanting to craft the most mind-blowing night Ashley had ever experienced. Paul opened the door to their room, and Ashley walked in, smiling as she glanced around and admired the decor. The hotel was a remnant of old New Orleans, with exposed brick walls, antique furniture, and an almost haunted feel. She hopped onto the bed, spreading her legs suggestively as she smiled broadly at her husband. "Oh, not yet, baby, you've got a *long* night of that to come," Paul laughed as he began to unpack their small overnight bag.

"So what exactly is happening tonight?" Ashley asked, tossing her shoes across the room and grabbing the remote to see what was on television. "Not to worry, I have a great night planned. Drop the remote and put this on, the party's about to start." Paul tossed her a bag from her favorite shop, Trashy Diva. Ashley peeked in and

238

grinned, already liking what she saw. She practically sprung off the bed, ran to the bathroom, and began to remove the items from the bag. There was a gorgeous black bustier that laced up the back, a matching g string, thigh high stockings, and a blindfold. A blindfold? Not exactly her thing, but she'd play along. For a while. Ashley quickly donned her new outfit, minus the blindfold, and opened the door just a crack, sliding a leg out suggestively and attempting not to laugh.

"Very nice," Paul complimented her. "Now let me see the *rest* of you." Ashley hopped out from behind the door, striking an exaggerated pose, but looking gorgeous nonetheless. The bustier complimented her ample breasts quite well, and her legs looked long and lean in the stockings and garters. She stood on tiptoes since she'd left her heels in the corner. Paul smiled as he delighted in the sight of his beautiful wife. She was perfect, even lovelier than the day he'd met her, and he absolutely adored her. He smiled as he pondered the events to come, and he checked his watch, realizing it was about time for his guests to arrive. Wanting to make the night as pleasurable as possible for her, Paul had carefully selected four men who were just her type, who seemed to have the body and

239

experience necessary to truly please her. He'd arranged for them to meet at the bar across the street, and he'd told them he would text when it was time to begin the evening's festivities.

Paul sent a quick text to one of the party guests, then he walked over to Ashley and put his arms around her, kissing her deeply. "I love you," he said softly, sliding his hand down her arm and grabbing the blindfold which she still held. "Put this on, and lie down on the bed." Ashley protested, but Paul wouldn't hear it, so she finally slipped on the blindfold with a loud sigh and assumed a sexy pose on the bed. Paul smiled. "That's my girl," he said with a laugh as he checked his watch and kept an eye on the door. Within a few minutes, he heard a soft knock. Party time.

Paul opened the door and put his finger up to his mouth, making it clear he wanted his guests to remain very quiet for the time being. In walked three extraordinarily attractive men, all of whom were dressed nicely and seemed eager to meet the guest of honor. Andrew was a surfer boy type, with dirty blond hair, a deep tan, and a sculpted body. Jonathan was next to come through the door; he was a college student, and while he looked a little nervous, he also looked like someone Ashley would drool over if they saw him out in public. He was pale and thin, but clearly had some muscles hiding under his clothes. Black glasses set off his features and made his ice blue eyes really stand out. Paul smiled as he thought about the two of them together, and what fun it would be to watch them. Tony was the last to enter; his olive complexion was similar to Ashley's, and he had a definite boy-next-door appeal. He smiled broadly at Paul and opened his mouth to greet him, but Paul quickly shushed him and pointed to the wall where he wanted the men to stand.

The three men stood next to the bed, admiring Paul's beautiful wife. Paul had been extremely clear with each of them that his wife was the most precious thing in the world to him, and that all he wanted was her happiness. He'd laid out the rules: they must use condoms, they weren't allowed to kiss her, they must play nicely with the other guests, and they must immediately stop if Ashley said no at any time. They all seemed to fully understand Paul's rules, and Paul was confident the night would be a rousing success for all involved. He knew Ashley would give them a run for their money, but he felt certain they could keep up. After giving them a moment to enjoy Ashley in her blindfolded state,

Paul told Ashley that the guests had arrived, and that she could take off the blindfold.

Ashley ripped the sash from her face in record time, and she put her hand over her mouth and giggled loudly when she saw what was waiting for her. She glanced over at Paul with a warm, loving smile, and she gave him a little wink. The men began to undress, and Ashley enjoyed the show. It was clear that Andrew and Tony enjoyed undressing in front of her; they drew it out and teased her as she bit her lip and watched the clothes come off. Jonathan seemed a bit shyer as he undressed, but once he stood there naked, he was every bit as impressive as his companions. Ashley sat at the edge of the bed, excited at the thought of being surrounded by gorgeous men as her husband looked on lovingly. Surprisingly, Jonathan was the first to approach her. She was glad he left his glasses on when he undressed; she found his school boy look incredibly sexy. Knowing kissing was forbidden, he walked up to her, ran his fingers through her hair, then guided her head down towards his already-erect cock. Ashley quickly slid down onto her back to get closer to him, and she ran her hands along the base of his shaft as she glided her lips across the tip. She licked and teased

242

him until he forced her head down, pushing his cock deep into her mouth. She sucked him hungrily, and he let out a groan as his cock swelled with pleasure.

Tony had walked up next to Jonathan, and Ashley looked up to see him stroking his cock as he watched them. The sight of his hand slowly and intently traveling up and down his rigid cock excited her, and she began to suck Jonathan harder and faster. She moaned as she worked Jonathan's cock, still enjoying the show Tony was putting on for her. She felt someone next to her and realized Andrew had sat on the bed next to her. He wasn't touching her in any way, but he watched the action intently, as if he was determining how he'd best join in. At that moment, Jonathan let out a guttural moan then pulled away from Ashley. He nodded to Tony, who eagerly took his place and guided his cock into Ashley's waiting mouth.

As Ashley worked on Tony's cock, Jonathan climbed onto the bed and slid between Ashley's legs, parting them and exploring her pussy with his fingers, gliding across her smooth, slick skin until he found her opening. She arched her back as his fingers entered her, and her chest heaved as he worked them in and out of her pussy, paying special attention to the spongy bundle of nerves buried inside her. Not wanting to be left out any longer, Andrew moved in next to Jonathan and leaned down to kiss Ashley's belly. His mouth trailed down to her smooth mound, and further down until he reached her swollen and extremely sensitive clit. He licked it softly as Jonathan continued plunging his fingers methodically into her. Ashley panted and gasped, a cock still in her mouth, and she reached out and pushed Andrew's head down, forcing him to lick her harder.

Her breathing grew heavier and heavier, and she released Tony's cock as she fell back onto the bed and began writhing with pleasure. Tony sat beside her and rubbed her breasts gently with one hand as he stroked his cock with the other. Ashley looked at her husband, who was sitting in a nearby chair, watching the show with a smile on his face. She smiled back at him, knowing how much he was enjoying what he saw, and knowing how much she would enjoy him later that night. As their eyes locked, with Jonathan's fingers buried in her pussy, Tony's hand on her breast, and Andrew's tongue caressing her clit, Ashley leapt off the bed in an explosive orgasm. The men continued working her over, and she shuddered with pleasure again and again until she finally let out a low

244

moan, grew still for a moment, then convulsed wildly as she came so hard she nearly tossed all three men off the bed.

Jonathan was the first to grab a condom from the nightstand, slip it on, and crawl between Ashley's legs. He slid his hands under her knees and pulled her towards him, then plunged his cock into her. Her body responded immediately, and she let out a long, low moan as she felt her pussy tighten again and again. Andrew knelt over her, guiding his cock into Ashley's mouth and fucking her face in rhythm with Jonathan's thrusts. Tony jerked off to the sight of her holes being filled, and as much as he'd wanted to fuck her himself, the scene was too much for him to bear, and he exploded all over her breasts. Andrew began to pound his cock almost violently into her mouth as he watched Jonathan slide in and out of her pussy. He reached down and rubbed her clit as she sucked him, and her mouth vibrated on his cock as she moaned. The sensation was incredible, and after a few more thrusts, he let out a loud grunt, pulled his cock out, and came all over her mouth and cheeks. He continued to rub her pussy as Jonathan fucked her, and her body once again tensed up, then convulsed as the pleasure overtook her. Jonathan grabbed her ankles and held her legs up so he could fuck her as deeply as possible, and as she cried out with pleasure, he began to almost growl as his cock swelled inside her. He pounded into her again and again, then finally let out a scream of pure ecstasy as he climaxed.

Ashley lay naked on the bed and watched the three men get dressed. Jonathan disappeared into the bathroom, returning with a wet towel and wiping off her face and chest. Ashley sat up, smiling and pulling the covers over herself as the guys thanked Paul and wished them both a great night. Paul locked the door, undressed quickly, and dove under the covers. He kissed Ashley slowly at first, then almost roughly, as he ran his hands up and down her silky soft back. "That was unbelievably hot," he whispered between kisses. "And now I have you all to myself. You're not too worn out for another go round, are you?" Ashley grinned wickedly at him. "Of course not," she replied as she threw off the covers and climbed on top of her husband, grabbing his cock and guiding it into her pussy. "I'm just getting started."

About the Author

Audra Morgan is a wife, mother, entrepreneur, writer, and possibly above all else, a submissive. Her own personal experiences and perspectives are woven throughout everything she writes. She is in the midst of writing several short stories on the topics of both swinging and BDSM. Her most recent publication is a short humorous memoir about her experiences with her husband in the swinging community. Turn the page for a sneak peek at chapter one!

Swinging by a Thread: The Misadventures of an Accidental Swinger

Prologue

I've read quite a few "memoirs" over the years which were quite obviously exaggerated to the point of becoming complete fiction, with only the smallest grains of truth scattered throughout. I'd like to point out, straight away, that this is not such a story. Much of the past five years of my life has fallen into the "truth is stranger than fiction" category, and a dear friend downright insisted I record my strange, but true, stories so that my life could serve as comic relief for someone other than her. At her behest, I've done so, and other than changing names to protect the far-from-innocent, all of the details in the pages before you are my own true, unembellished life experiences. In fact, they're so accurate that I'm bound to get an angry email or two from people who recognize the stories a bit too well! Still, I felt compelled to tell these stories, and to keep it real. For some of you, it will serve simply as the means to

248

a good laugh. For others, it may hit close to home, reminding you of some of your own funny experiences. For others still, it may even spur you on to create some adventures of your own. And if you do that, I hope to read about them one day – I could use a laugh that isn't at my own expense!

Chapter One

How It Began, or Always Blame the Bartender

This is the story of five years of crazy adventures in swinging, and of some of the things I've learned through our more outrageous encounters. You don't know me from Jack, so I'm not going to bore you with a twenty page background on my life. Still, I think context is pretty fundamental, so let me begin with a little bit about *us*, and about how we ended up on this path.

Tyler and I spent the first ten years of our relationship being homebodies. He was never much for going out; he preferred a quiet night at home, watching movies or playing games. I, on the other hand, had to adjust to the quiet life. I'd spent my years in college and grad school partying almost nightly, and my new, quieter life was a big change, to say the least. I grew used to it, though, and then once we had kids, it became a no brainer that nightlife from there on out would involve falling asleep watching Saturday Night Live together. Yes, the all-too-typical routine of being married with kids. With that routine, though, came a serious emotional and sexual rut in our relationship. For a while, we both assumed this was the natural progression of marriage; it seemed everyone we knew was going through the same thing, so we didn't discuss it, much less attempt to fix it. It just *was*. At some point, we thankfully agreed that our relationship was worth more than that, that we were *better* than that, and we began making a conscious effort to change things for the better.

For our ninth anniversary, Tyler surprised me with a night out which consisted of an amazing hotel room, dinner, and a fun night at my favorite bar from my college days. It felt so good to get out again, to be around people drinking and laughing and having fun. I felt like I'd come home, and Tyler could see how happy I was. From that point on, we made going out at least once a month a priority. We settled into a wonderful new routine of meeting our friends, mostly the parents of our kids' friends, for cocktails and dancing and general absurdity. Monthly nights out turned into twice-a-month gatherings, and those nights were soon supplemented with drunken game nights and movie nights. We were truly having more fun than we'd ever had before, and our marriage was all the stronger for it. Then, one night, a bartender at that very same bar told us a story that, quite honestly, changed our lives forever.

Gene, our favorite bartender, smiled broadly as we entered the bar one Saturday night. He made us our drinks before we even reached our barstools; we were pretty predictable. As he placed our drinks down on the bar, he leaned forward and began to tell us about his adventures the previous night. "Guys, I have to tell you about this club I went to with a friend last night. It was insane. Naked people everywhere. Having sex! I've never seen anything like it. You guys should check it out, you would die!" Before he could tell us more, he was called to the other side of the bar, and that was the last we spoke to him that night.

Now, I've never even been to a strip club in my life, it just holds no interest for me; I'm a naturally curious person, though, and it intrigued me that this place existed in my city. This club with regular people who got naked and had sex in front of each other. Did these places really exist outside porn and bad Tom Cruise movies? What kind of people would go to such a place? Had Gene been exaggerating, as I suspected he sometimes did when telling stories? The next morning, despite my hangover, I was up early, searching online for answers to my questions.

"Did you know we had a swingers club here?" I asked Tyler incredulously. He'd heard a coworker talk about it once, but he didn't really get any details. I still couldn't quite fathom it. Unfortunately, what we could find online just didn't quench our thirst for details about this club that had been operating for nearly ten years mere minutes from our house. While I'd never had any desire to set foot in a strip club, I suddenly felt a need to have a glimpse into this secret world where things happened that I had to admit I couldn't even really imagine. Regular people, exposing their bodies and their sex lives to others, not for money, but for the sheer enjoyment of it. I felt like the most sheltered, naive person in the world, and I felt the overwhelming desire to unburden myself of that naiveté.

Now, let me make one thing clear, in case you weren't paying attention: Tyler and I were not, had never been, and had never considered being, swingers. We'd been monogamous, with no exceptions, for our entire marriage, and we had no intentions of changing that. That being said, we both felt drawn to this mysterious club, simply so we could see what went on there, and so we could be "in the know" about this secret place that apparently did not even have a sign on the door or a listing in the phone book. We quickly realized that if we were going to learn anything

253

about this place before actually stepping foot in the door, we'd have to make contact with people online and get information first-hand.

We emailed a few people who had posted in online forums about the club; we made it clear that we were just going as visitors, to check the place out, and that we wanted to learn more about it before we actually went. A very nice couple replied to our email, told us all about the club, and assured us that people are more than welcome to just go, have a few drinks, check out what was happening, and leave without having to worry about being accosted in any way. In fact, they pointed out, we were more likely to be hit on inappropriately at any random bar than at a swing club. Who knew! This couple was from out of town, but they'd been to the club many times before; they offered to meet us a few blocks away at a neighborhood bar, walk us to the club (since it was somewhat difficult to find), and show us around. We appreciated their kindness and generosity, and we made plans for that weekend. We agreed we were going simply to drink, people watch, and learn a little about this completely different way of life.

To read the rest of this humorous and completely true account of swinging-often-gone-awry, please look for

Swinging by a Thread: The Misadventures of an Accidental Swinger, available exclusively on Amazon.

Printed in Great Britain
by Amazon